Playing games . . .

"Well, excuuuse me, *Nicky!*" Jonathan shouted. "Forgive me for forgetting about a stupid girls' soccer game!"

Quinn whipped around. "What did you say?" she asked.

"It's only a girls' soccer game," he repeated loudly. "It's nothing to get excited about!"

"Of course it is!" Alicia screamed. "It's the first State Championship in school history!"

"A *girls'* championship?" Jonathan said sarcastically. "Give me a break."

"What do you mean by that?" Quinn asked, fuming. How could this guy make her want to kill him one minute, and she didn't-know-what the next?

"Come on, Quinn," Jonathan said, angry too. "You know that soccer is a boys' game. Girls can't play it as well. It's like any other sport."

"We'll have to see about that," Quinn replied, suddenly calm.

"What's that supposed to mean?" Jonathan asked.

"You'll see," Quinn retorted.

"Her friends looked worried. When Quinn's moods changed this suddenly, it was never a good sign. She was definitely up to something . . .

Tor Books Presents the Palm Beach Prep series

Developed by Elle Wolfe

Lonely Heart by E. M. Rees
The Real Scoop by Susan Booker
The Girls Against the Boys by Susan Booker
Screen Test by Susan Smith*

*Forthcoming

THE GIRLS AGAINST THE BOYS

Developed by
Elle Wolfe

A TOM DOHERTY ASSOCIATES BOOK
NEW YORK

THE GIRLS AGAINST THE BOYS

Copyright © 1990 by Angel Entertainment, Inc.

A Tor Book
Published by Tom Doherty Associates, Inc.
49 West 24th Street
New York, N.Y. 10010

Cover art by Richard Lauter

ISBN: 0-812-51063-1

First edition: October 1990

Printed in the United States of America

0 9 8 7 6 5 4 3 2 1

CHAPTER 1

"There's only one minute left!" Esme Farrell yelled as she jumped up and down on the sideline of the soccer field. "Just one more goal!" she shouted louder than before, if that was possible. She grabbed Nicole Whitcomb, who was standing with her, and looked over at the scoreboard, groaning at what she saw: PALM BEACH PREP—3, ORLANDO DAY—3. The teams had been tied for the whole last quarter and the PBP girls were running out of time. "They have to get a goal," Esme said to Nicole, brushing one of her blonde braids back over her shoulder.

"Help out, help out!" Vanessa Robb shouted from her position at fullback. Two Orlando Day forwards were bearing down on her with the ball between them. Stephanie Barnes saw that Vanessa was in trouble and raced back from the center of the field

1

to come up behind the Orlando Day girls. She intercepted the next pass and chipped the ball up to her front line. Quinn McNair, the center forward, was already racing toward the ball before it landed. Her wing, Alicia Antona, and Stephanie, the center halfback, raced alongside to give her support.

"Go Quinn!" Avery Holmes shouted from the side of the field. The PBP English teacher was completely into the game. He was standing with Candy Gordon, who taught history and horseback riding. They were jumping up and down and cheering almost as loudly as the girls in the stands.

"C'mon, Quinn," Candy Gordon added. "Stomp on 'em!" After she said it, she felt Avery's eyes on her, and turned to see him staring at her strangely.

"Stomp on them?" he repeated, his attention drawn away from the action on the field. "Don't you think that's a little violent, Candy? We want the girls to win, but we don't want to teach victory at any cost, do we?" he teased.

"Right," she answered, embarrassed, not realizing he was kidding. "I guess I got a little carried away. But this *is* the State Championship, you know."

"I just think we should all try to keep this in perspective, that's all," Avery said as seriously as he could. "It is, after all, only a soccer game." He paused, then saw Quinn fake out one of Orlando's halfbacks and get that much closer to the goal. "Stomp on 'em!" he shouted, and then turned to see Candy's shocked expression. They both laughed, before shifting their attention back to the game.

Meanwhile, Quinn was determined that this drive

would end in a goal. A few pieces of her thick red hair clung to her forehead and she pushed them back impatiently as she worked the ball further down the field. She could hear Stephanie yelling, "Pass, pass," right behind her, while Alicia kept up with her on her right. They *were* going to get this goal.

Just then, the Orlando center halfback appeared right in front of Quinn. Quinn tried to dribble around her, but the girl stayed right in front of her. Knowing that it was just a matter of seconds before she was tackled, Quinn passed back to Stephanie. Then she was around the halfback searching for an open position. The halfback wouldn't give up, though, and stuck to her like glue. Stephanie's cry of "Help out" caught Quinn's attention, and she saw that Stephanie had a real problem. The Orlando Day left fullback was bearing in on her, full speed. And the girl was really big. Quinn couldn't shake her shadow to help Stephanie out, so she faked to the outside, leaving the middle wide open. Alicia took advantage of it, and moved quickly in front of the goal, with only the right fullback between her and the goalie.

"Pass it to Alicia!" Esme screamed as she ran along the sidelines, trying to keep up with the play. Nicole was right beside her screaming for PBP to get a goal. Her normally neat brown ponytail was disheveled as she glanced up at the clock. "Fifteen seconds!" she screamed. "C'mon guys! You can do it!"

Stephanie dribbled to the side, trying to escape the large fullback, and then seeing it was no use, spotted Alicia open in the middle. She chipped the ball over the fullback, placing it in front of the goal. Alicia watched the ball as it flew toward the goal, and raced under it. As it descended, Alicia got ready. They had certainly practiced this move enough during the last week. The Orlando Day goalie made the mistake of looking at Alicia's feet, waiting for the ball to hit the ground. It never did. Alicia headed it over the surprised goalie. The referee's whistle blew and the final buzzer sounded at the same time.

"Goal!" the ref shouted needlessly above the pandemonium that had erupted on and off the field. The PBP team swarmed around Alicia. Quinn reached her first and hugged her, picking her up. Stephanie barreled into them from behind, and they all started jumping up and down. Soon it was just a mass of bodies—jumping, hugging, and squealing in excitement. They were Middle School State Champs! Unbelievable. Quinn threw her cleats up into the air in excitement. Then she led a group of ecstatic girls over to the bench—and the water cooler. Before Coach Larsen knew what hit her, Quinn, Stephanie, and Alicia had dumped the entire contents of the water cooler over her head. Then everyone was hugging her.

"Great job, girls!" Coach screamed, brushing her wet hair out of her face.

When the PBP team was a bit more controlled, they went over to the Orlando Day bench where the players were quietly pulling on their sweat suits. A few of them held towels up to their faces to hide their tears. After Quinn and Alicia had shaken the hand of every Orlando Day girl, they raced over to their sideline, where Nicole and Esme were dancing around in circles.

"Way to go, guys!" Esme shouted as they all ran together in a group hug. "Great shot, Lish!"

"Yeah, we'll have to call you Pelé Antona from now on," Nicole joked.

"I can't believe it!" Alicia exclaimed. "I saw you heading down the field, Quinn, and I just thought I'd better follow. I knew we didn't have much time left when Stephanie got into trouble. That was great the way you cleared out the middle."

"Well, I didn't know what else to do," Quinn answered, breathlessly. "I couldn't shake that half-back. I knew we had to get a goal. I don't think I could have lasted an overtime."

"I know," Alicia panted. "I thought my lungs were about to burst. Wasn't Stephanie's pass amazing? Where is she anyway?"

All the girls turned to see Stephanie still over at the Orlando Day bench. She seemed to be arguing with the large fullback who had blocked her path. "What's going on?" Alicia asked curiously.

"Well, after Stephanie passed you that ball, Lish, that fullback totally flattened her!" Esme explained. "Even though she didn't have the ball anymore!"

"I think we'd better go over there," Quinn suggested. The four girls headed back toward their opponents' bench. But the Orlando Day coach had intervened before they reached it, and Stephanie was on her way back. The girls met her midfield.

"I can't believe that girl!" Stephanie said angrily, her dark eyes flashing. "Just because we won, she had to pull that. We're better soccer players, and better sportsmen!"

"That's sports*women*," Quinn reminded her. Stephanie laughed.

"Hey, we did it! We won!" Stephanie shouted, as if she had just remembered.

"Great pass, Steph!" Alicia praised her, patting her back as they walked across the field together.

"Great goal, Lish."

"Great setup, Quinn."

"Great game, guys."

The five of them broke up laughing. "Here we are, the mutual admiration society!" Quinn exclaimed.

Mr. Holmes and Ms. Gordon were waiting for them on the sidelines.

"Great game, team!" Mr. Holmes congratulated them.

"You guys were terrific!" Ms. Gordon added as she hugged each girl. She was one of their favorite teachers, and they were happy to accept her praise. "That was some totally awesome footwork out there, Quinn," she added. The girls giggled. They couldn't get over it when their teachers, even their favorite ones, used words like "awesome."

"Thanks, Ms. Gordon," Quinn said, practically beaming. "The team works so well together, I knew there was no way we could lose."

Mr. Holmes started to say something else, but just then Quinn's three brothers attacked her. Sean, her sixteen-year-old brother, picked her up and swung her around and around. Patrick, her youngest brother, just keep shouting "Yahoo!" over and over again, and Brian, who was ten, kept trying to grab Quinn. Finally, Sean stopped and the three of them jumped on Quinn. For a full five minutes, it was utter chaos. Finally, things slowed down a little when Mr. and Mrs. McNair joined them. Of course it got crazy again as the huge Antona clan converged on the girls. Mr. Holmes and Ms. Gordon tried to sneak away amidst all the congratulations. Quinn stopped them.

"Thanks for coming to watch!" she called out. "We really appreciate the support."

"Are you kidding?" Ms. Gordon asked, incredulously. "I wouldn't have missed this for the world. It's not every day PBP plays a State Championship match, let alone wins it."

"Hey, even Mrs. Hartman was impressed," Mr. Holmes said. Quinn looked disbelieving. She and Mrs. Hartman, the headmistress of PBP, had had their share of difficulties. "I actually saw her jumping up and down a little in the bleachers," he added.

"No way!" Quinn exclaimed.

"I don't believe it!" Alicia added. "I didn't think she ever left PBP."

"Well, there were plenty of witnesses," Mr. Holmes assured them, his brown eyes twinkling. All the girls were flattered that he was paying so much attention to them. He was, without a doubt, the most gorgeous teacher they had ever had.

"So, maybe she's not so bad after all," Quinn countered, teasing him. "She really *is* human."

He laughed. He and Ms. Gordon said congratulations one more time, and then they left.

The girls all looked at each other, and Quinn shrugged. "I don't know, you tell me," she said.

"Well, they did *leave* together," Alicia said.

"And they spent the whole game *standing* together," Esme added. They were always speculating on whether or not Mr. Holmes and Ms. Gordon were dating. As everyone's favorite teachers at PBP, and the youngest, Ms. Gordon and Mr. Holmes seemed destined for each other—at least in the girls' minds. The girls never stopped trying to arrange something between them.

"Hey, who cares today?" Nicole suddenly exclaimed. "You guys are STATE CHAMPS!" Then, they were all screaming again.

"Stephanie, come on!" a voice ordered from behind them.

Everyone turned around to see, to no one's surprise, Cara Knowles. Cara fancied herself the queen of the sixth grade. Stephanie was one of her good friends. Even though Alicia, Nicole, Esme, and Quinn didn't get along with Cara, Stephanie was well liked. "Come on, Steph," Cara repeated. "We don't want to be late for dinner."

Stephanie turned to the others and apologized. "I'm sorry, guys. I promised Cara we would go out to dinner tonight. I've got to go." Everyone congratulated her again, and then she trotted off.

"Mom, that's a great idea!" Quinn said. "Why don't we all go out to dinner and celebrate?"

"Dinner? Food?" Esme asked, excitedly. Even though she was a professional model, Esme ate all the time. She was like a vacuum cleaner. Quinn had taken to calling her "Hoover" when they went out to eat. "Let me call my mom," Esme added. "Maybe she'll want to meet us."

"Dinner's a great idea, Quinn," Mr. McNair said.

"What do you say?" he asked the Antonas. They agreed, and the Antonas and the McNairs said they'd meet the girls in the parking lot after their showers. Then they'd head over to Luigi's, an Italian restaurant in Nueva Beach.

The four girls walked toward the locker room. Esme wanted to race. "Last one there is a pair of smelly sweat socks!" she yelled as she took off. Nicole jogged after her. Her mother and new stepfather were in New York, so she wanted to call her grandparents and let them know where'd she be. Alicia and Quinn walked slowly to the showers. They were dead tired from the game, and hungry enough to eat a horse—but they were wearing two of the biggest smiles in Palm Beach. They were State Champs!

CHAPTER 2

"I still can't believe you won," Esme said the next day, as she ran circles around her friends, pretending to dribble and head the ball. "You two were totally amazing!"

Esme, Nicole, Alicia, and Quinn had just parked their bikes in Nicole's driveway and were on their way up to her room.

"The whole team was totally amazing!" Quinn countered, as she flung open Nicole's door and threw herself on the bed. Nicole had taken to keeping her door closed all the time now since her new stepbrother, Jonathan, had moved in. It wasn't that she thought he would steal something, but Nicole felt her privacy threatened with two new people in the house. She wanted to keep her room her own.

Alicia plopped down next to Quinn. She let her head and shoulders fall off the side of the bed, allowing the blood to rush to her brain. "Yeah, but I don't think my body will ever be the same again!"

"I know what you mean," Quinn agreed, stretching her leg over her head. "My muscle aches have aches. I feel like an old lady with arthritis."

Esme began pretending she was a really old lady, and started walking around the room all hunched over. "Soon we'll be visiting you at the Senior Center," she teased in a quavery voice.

"Right. And we'll play shuffleboard together, and then rub Ben-Gay on our sore muscles," Quinn teased back.

"But it was worth it, wasn't it?" Nicole asked. "I mean Palm Beach Prep is the State Champ, right?"

"Definitely!" Alicia said emphatically. "And that article in the *Palm Beach Sentinel* wasn't too bad either."

"The picture was kind of goofy, though," Quinn said. A quick reporter had gotten a great shot of Quinn, Alicia, and Stephanie jumping on each other after Alicia made the winning goal.

"I think it was an awesome picture because it wasn't posed," Esme countered. "It looked totally *real*."

"Yeah, real goofy," Alicia said, giggling.

"Well, the article wasn't too bad," Nicole offered. She pulled open the bottom drawer of her dresser and started searching for her swimsuit.

"No . . ." Quinn began.

"Oh no, the professional critique," Alicia teased. Quinn wanted to be a writer, and as the author of

"The Real Scoop" column in the *Sixth Gator*, PBP's sixth-grade newspaper, she tended to criticize articles in every paper.

"Well, you have to admit that some of the articles written about our soccer team this year made it sound like it was just totally amazing that girls could even *play* sports, let alone win at them," Quinn put in, a little angrily.

"That's true," Nicole agreed. "It makes me so mad sometimes, like when I'm the "girl rider" at shows. I mean, I'm just a rider."

"Right," Alicia agreed. "We're *athletes* on the soccer team first, and then girls."

"But, those articles always refer to us as "girl athletes," Quinn said, sitting up and searching through her bag for her new bathing suit. "Why do they have to write about us differently from the way they write about the guys?"

"I don't know," Esme said, distractedly. She was trying to tie her new lime-green and fuchsia bathing suit top, and couldn't see around to her back to check if she was doing it right. "Are we going to go swimming, or what?"

Nicole, already dressed in her pink and white striped one-piece, took the bathing suit strings from Esme, and tied them in a bow. "You're so impatient, Es. The water will still be there when we get out."

Quinn found her new blue bathing suit, and was struggling into it, when Esme and Alicia gasped.

"What?" Quinn asked, trying to get the right strap over her shoulder.

"That's not black!" Esme exclaimed. Alicia just nodded in agreement.

"Good observation," Quinn commented, dryly. "It's blue. You guys are really good with colors, you know."

"But you always wear a black bathing suit, Quinn," Alicia said, ignoring Quinn's sarcasm. "Why the change?"

"Well, my mom bought me this new suit, and my black one was kind of raggedy, so . . ." Quinn trailed off. "Why? You don't like it?"

"Oh, no!" Esme reassured her. "It looks great! We're just not used to it."

"Hey, let's get out to the pool, guys," Alicia said, pulling a white T-shirt over her neon orange bikini. "It's going to be dark at this rate."

"You're so impatient, Lish," Esme mimicked Nicole. Nicole grinned.

"Last one to the pool is a total dweeb!" Alicia screamed as she ran out of the room.

The other three girls looked at each other, and then took off in a mad rush after Alicia.

After they had all spread their towels out on the lounges by the pool, Nicole ran back inside to make some iced tea.

"And bring some cookies, or something!" Esme called after her, as she carefully applied her suntan lotion. Esme had really fair skin and burned easily, so her agent was always telling her to be careful in the sun. Putting all her different lotions on seemed to take forever. She had different types for her legs, her face, her hands, and the rest of her body. And if she went swimming, she had to put it all on again. It drove her friends crazy. They just tried to ignore her.

"Hey, Hoover, can you throw some of that lotion over here?" Quinn called.

Esme pretended to pout at her new nickname, then asked, "Which one?"

Quinn sighed. "Just the regular, ordinary kind. You do have that kind, don't you?"

Esme started looking at the backs of all her bottles, and shrugged.

Alicia laughed. "Here, Quinn," she offered, tossing her a bottle. "You can have some of mine."

"Thanks." Esme went back to her almost-scientific application of lotion. By the time Quinn had finished covering herself with Coppertone, Nicole was back with snacks.

"Oh, thank goodness!" Esme exclaimed. "I was beginning to feel dehydrated. And starved!"

Everyone laughed. Alicia leaned over and scooped some water out of the pool to throw at Esme.

"Hey!" Esme yelled, jumping up and shaking herself off.

"Oh, sorry. My hand slipped," Alicia said, giggling.

"Sure, Lish. Now I have to put all that lotion back on again."

Everyone groaned.

"I was thinking of starting on that history paper tonight," Nicole said a few moments later, after some silent moments of sun-soaking.

"Nicole, that's not due for ages!" Esme exclaimed. She couldn't understand Nicole sometimes. She started assignments long before they were due, and even studied for several days before quizzes.

"I know," Nicole answered, a little defensively. "But I want to do well on it."

"That's okay, Nicole," Quinn reassured her. Quinn admired her friend's study habits. Quinn got good grades, too, but she wasn't a straight-A student like Nicole, except in English. "I should start mine soon, too."

Quinn stood up, and headed toward the diving board. Sean was teaching her how to do flips, and she practiced every time she was swimming at Nicole's.

"WAAATCH OOOUUT!!!"

Quinn jumped back, out of the way, as Jonathan came whizzing toward the pool on his skateboard. Jonathan was in the seventh grade at G. Adams Prep, Palm Beach Prep's brother school. Quinn had seen him a lot since Nicole's mother remarried, and he moved down here from New York. She didn't know why, but every time she saw him, she was speechless, and her whole body got hot all over. She really admired the fact that he never gave in to pressure to be like everybody else, and was just himself. Quinn, also, never did anything just because everyone else was doing it. Sometimes even her friends thought she was a little weird. But they knew that Quinn marched to the beat of her own drummer. The problem was, she could never tell Jonathan any of these things. She couldn't understand why not. She had three brothers, and they had lots of friends who were always over, and she was friends with a lot of G. Adams guys. She never had any trouble talking to any of them. So why Jonathan?

Jonathan skidded his skateboard to a stop right at

the edge of the pool, but couldn't stop his forward momentum. He went flying into the pool, getting the girls all wet—especially Quinn since she was closest. As he pulled himself out, Nicole started yelling at him.

"You got us all wet! What's wrong with you! Why don't you watch where you're going! Look at Quinn! She's soaked!"

Jonathan stopped shaking out his longish black hair, and pulled it back into a ponytail. He turned toward Quinn, his silver hoop earring glinting in the late afternoon sun.

"Hey, sorry about that, Quinn," he apologized. "I couldn't stop myself from falling. My dad says I'm going to kill myself on this skateboard one day."

Quinn felt her whole body get hot again, with him looking straight at her like that. "It's okay," she managed to get out in a soft voice. "I was just about to go in anyway."

"Oh, yeah, Quinn," Alicia said. "Aren't you going to show us that flip or whatever it was that Sean just taught you?"

Now she was really on the spot. Jonathan didn't look like he was going to leave anytime soon, and she didn't really want to dive in front of him. What was her problem? What was the big deal anyway?

"Jonathan, try to be more careful on that stupid skateboard, okay?" Nicole went on, as if she hadn't heard his apology to Quinn.

"Hey, I'm sorry, *Nicky*," he said with an irritating grin on his face.

"That's Nicole," she answered through clenched teeth. "You know I hate to be called Nicky." Jonathan could be so irritating sometimes. She knew that he called her Nicky just to irritate her. Most of the time, he was obnoxious and he acted as if he owned the place. Sometimes, he wasn't so bad, even if he did listen to heavy metal. What he saw in Living Colour and Guns N' Roses was beyond her. It was head-banging kind of music, even if Esme did listen to "Appetite for Destruction" sometimes when she cleaned her room. Nicole was always telling Jonathan to turn his stereo down, because his music made the whole second floor of the house vibrate. He was also really lazy when it came to studying. She couldn't understand how he could get decent grades when she never even saw him with a book. That made her really mad sometimes.

"Sorry, *Nicole*," Jonathan apologized, stressing "Nicole." "I really couldn't stop. So, like, what are you girls doing?" He got back on his skateboard and started riding all around the patio, trying to flip the board under his feet. He spent a lot of time circling Quinn. Quinn didn't know where to look, or what to say. "What about that flip, Quinn?" he asked. "I'd really like to see it."

Quinn really didn't know what to do now. She guessed that she had no choice but to dive. Why was this so embarrassing for her anyway? She walked over to the diving board.

Jonathan flipped his skateboard up, catching it in his hand, and walked over to Alicia. "Who's Sean anyway?" he asked, under his breath. Alicia peered over her sunglasses at him. "Her brother," she answered, wondering why in the world he had asked her that.

Then Quinn walked to the end of the board, and turned around. Facing backwards, she jumped back and did a forward flip toward the board. Her hair flapped against the end of the diving board. She entered the water feet first.

Esme gasped. "Oh my gosh!"

"She was so close!" Nicole exclaimed.

Quinn surfaced, and everyone started yelling at her. "You almost hit the diving board, Quinn!" Alicia yelled.

Quinn laughed. "Sean says the closer you get, the better it is. Not that you should try to hit it or anything, but you don't want to be too far away," she explained as she paddled to the side.

"That was way cool, Quinn!" Jonathan said admiringly. "Could you teach me how to do that?" he asked, as he extended a hand toward her to help her out of the pool.

"Sure," she agreed, flustered to be touching him, as he pulled her up. When she stood up she was very close to him, but he didn't step back.

"Hey, did you read the article in the paper?" Esme asked, breaking Quinn's trance. Quinn walked over to her towel and picked it up to dry herself off, while Jonathan turned to Esme.

"What article?" he asked.

"The one about the soccer team, Jonathan," Nicole said sharply. "Remember? I told you last night that PBP beat Orlando Day yesterday and won the State Championship."

"Oh, yeah," Jonathan said, as if remembering a not-very-important fact. "Right. The State Championship."

Nicole didn't let up on him. "Just because you've never been on a State Championship team doesn't mean that you have to act like that!"

"I just forgot! I'm sorry, Nicole," Jonathan tried to apologize.

"You did not! You knew that PBP won the championship! Don't try to act dumb!" Nicole started raising her voice now. Her three friends stared at her. She was always a little on edge whenever Jonathan was around, but they had never seen her act like this before.

"Well, excuuuse me, *Nicky*!" Jonathan shouted back, finally goaded into it. "Forgive me for forgetting about a stupid girls' soccer game!"

Quinn whipped around. "What did you say?" she asked, in a tight voice.

"It's only a girls' soccer game," he repeated loudly. "It's nothing to get excited about!"

"Of course it is! It's the first State Championship in school history!" Alicia pointed out.

"A *girls'* championship?" Jonathan said sarcastically. "Give me a break."

"What do you mean by that?" Quinn asked, fuming. How could this guy make her want to kill him one minute, and she didn't-know-what the next?

"Come on, Quinn," Jonathan said, angry too. "You know that soccer is a boys' game. Girls can't play it as well. It's like any other sport."

"That is totally ludicrous!" Quinn yelled back. "You don't know what you're talking about. That kind of thinking went out with the Stone Age. We are as good as any boys' team!"

Jonathan guffawed. "Please Quinn. Spare me. The

Feminist Movement went out in the sixties. Keep up with the times."

Quinn took a deep breath to steady herself. She knew she was about to lose control, and there was nothing she could do about it. "When was the last time G. Adams won a State Championship in anything?"

Jonathan looked taken aback. "Hey, I just got to the school. It's not my fault. Besides, just because we haven't won some dumb trophy doesn't mean we're not good," he protested. "We were 10-3, and our front line is practically unstoppable."

"And you're on the front line, right?" Nicole asked, sarcastically.

"I *did* have twelve goals this season," he bragged. "Can any of you say that?"

"Yeah, but can you say that you scored the winning goal in a State Championship match either?" Quinn asked, pointing at Alicia. "I don't think so."

Jonathan shrugged, but didn't back down.

"So basically, you're saying that guys are better athletes than girls, right?" Quinn asked, seething.

"You said it, not me. Everyone knows it's true."

Quinn was so mad that she thought she was about to explode. She was so infuriated. What was with this guy? Esme saw the expression on Quinn's face, and knew there was going to be trouble. Quinn never got that look unless something made her really mad.

"So," Quinn began, in a cold, controlled voice. "You think if girls and boys played against each other in a soccer game, the boys would win?"

"Of course," Jonathan answered confidently.

"How can you even ask me that? But it's a stupid question because the guys never play the girls."

"Why not?" Quinn asked challengingly. "Are they scared to?"

"What do you mean?" Jonathan asked, confused. "We're not *scheduled* to play girls."

"Well, now that the season is over, it wouldn't be too difficult to have a game between G. Adams and PBP, would it?"

"What?!" Jonathan exclaimed. "We'd whale on you girls! You wouldn't know what hit you! It would be totally one-sided!"

"You really think so?" Quinn asked calmly. She was still mad, but now she had Jonathan exactly where she wanted him—maybe.

"Aside from the fact that we're bigger, stronger, and faster," Jonathan teased, "it would be a *totally* fair game. Maybe we could play with one leg and one arm tied behind our backs." He laughed, and walked over to the plate of cookies Nicole had brought out.

Quinn looked at her friends and smiled calmly. They were a bit nervous when Quinn started getting calm, but they relaxed when they saw what she was up to.

"So, why don't we have a challenge match, then?" she asked Jonathan as he turned around, his mouth full of cookies.

"That trophy really went to your head, didn't it?" he answered, wiping the crumbs off his face.

"You're not afraid we'll *beat* you, are you?" Alicia asked, goading him.

"No way!" Jonathan exclaimed. "Not even if we

played blindfolded.''

"C'mon soccer star, say yes, then,'' Quinn said, trying to control her excitement. She knew they had a really good chance against the guys. G. Adams was a good team, but not great, and they certainly didn't seem any taller, stronger, or faster than the girls, the way Jonathan said they were. The challenge game would show Jonathan that girls could be as good as boys in sports. Though why it was so important for Jonathan to know, was a mystery to her.

"Fine!'' he finally said. "I mean, I'll have to ask the rest of the team before it's definite.''

"No problem. I have to talk to the rest of our team, too. But I'm sure they'll want the opportunity to totally cream you guys. We can discuss where and when we'll have the game later!''

"Sure,'' he answered. "I'll go call my co-captain to work on strategy—like whether to beat you by five goals, or six!'' And with that, he was on his skateboard, speeding up the path to the house.

CHAPTER 3

"I can't believe he said that only guys can play soccer!" Stephanie exclaimed in disbelief, slamming her lunch tray in anger. "What is wrong with that guy anyway?" Then she looked at Nicole, who was sitting across the table. "No offense, Nicole. I know he's your stepbrother and all, but what a total jerk!"

Nicole just nodded her head, as if she agreed with Stephanie, and turned her attention back to her tuna sandwich. She was actually feeling a little weird about this whole thing. Quinn had called a meeting at lunch to let the sixth-grade members of the soccer team know about the big challenge game. Of course, Nicole agreed that everything Jonathan had said was truly infuriating, but she felt weird that everyone was discussing him like this. It was strange

23

to listen to the soccer team talk about what a dweeb her brother was—her stepbrother, that is.

Meanwhile, Quinn was thrilled that everyone was backing her on this challenge game. For her, it seemed kind of personal, and she had been worried that other people wouldn't be into it. But that morning, when she talked to Vanessa Robb and Darcy Chapin, the seventh-grade co-captains, they had liked the idea. Vanessa, in fact, had said that she wanted to put those chauvinistic pigs at G. Adams in their place once and for all. She and Darcy were going to tell all the seventh-graders on the soccer team, and they asked Quinn to hold a meeting at lunch.

"We're going to have to do some killer workouts this week to beat those guys," Quinn said, apologetically.

"Seriously," Virginia Choy said. "It's going to take a lot of work. I went to some of the G. Adams games this year with my brother, and Jonathan Stanton is an amazing player. And you should see their goalie—"

"Hey, let's not lose this game before we even play it," Stephanie cut in. "We *are* the State Champions, after all."

"Right," Quinn agreed, sitting down again. It looked as if this game was actually going to take place. "Remember, *they* didn't even make it through the first round of the playoffs. We have a great shot at beating them. Just because they're guys doesn't mean anything, right?"

"I agree," Stephanie affirmed. "Jonathan Stanton is such a throwback—thinking that men are superi-

or to women and all that."

"Really," Virginia agreed. "He's totally wacked out."

"Well, at least not *all* guys think like that," Esme put in. "Most of the guys, even on the team, are really nice."

"And Esme would know," Quinn joked, and everyone laughed. Esme knew a lot of guys at G. Adams, and the girls like to tease her about it.

"Well, Quinn," Esme teased back. "You know as many of them as I do, so you know I'm right."

A loud "oooohhh!" went up from the table as the girls acknowledged Esme's retaliation, and Mr. Holmes, the teacher on duty, headed over to see what was happening.

"What's going on, girls?" he asked, biting into an apple. "This looks like a soccer meeting. Isn't soccer over?"

The girls all looked up at his words. Most of them became speechless around him because they all had crushes on him.

"Well, Mr. Holmes," Quinn began confidently. She had no problem talking to him because she loved English, and she spent a lot of time in his office getting advice on writing or just talking about books. "See, this guy on the G. Adams team told us that a girls' State Championship isn't really that big a deal, because everyone knows that girls can't really play soccer. So we challenged the G. Adams team to a game." She paused, wondering what he would say to that. Sometimes she couldn't predict how he would react to things.

To everyone's surprise, he laughed. "That's terrific!" he exclaimed. "You really put those boys in their place. You know, you *are* women of the nineties!"

The girls looked relieved. Then, someone called Mr. Holmes from a few tables down, and he walked away.

"You know, this will be a good opportunity to ask some of the guys to that Sadie Hawkins dance," Nina Ellis said. "I mean, not to change the subject or anything, but I haven't asked anyone yet, and—"

"And you've been to the mall at least three times to pick out something to wear, and you need a date to justify a new outfit . . ." Nina's best friend, Chelsea, teased.

"I have not!" Nina retorted. "I've only been there twice."

Everyone laughed, and they all started talking at once about the dance, forgetting about the soccer game for a moment.

"Well, who are you going to ask?"

"Did you hear that Anne Marie Hayes asked Oliver Chubb to the dance, and he said no?!"

"Yeah, but then she asked Zach Burnett, and he said yes."

"Well, he's kind of cute."

"He's so funny, too."

"Not as funny as Gibby, though."

"Has anyone asked him yet?"

"No, I don't think so. Why? Do you want to ask him?"

"What? With a name like William Gibson Harris III? Please!"

"I heard Cara was thinking about asking a seventh-grader."

"Is that true? Would she really do that? Who?"

"I heard maybe Tommy Reed."

"No way! Do you think he'll go with her?"

"What about Jonathan?"

Quinn suddenly started paying attention to the conversation. She had tuned out after Mr. Holmes left.

"What about him?" she asked, kind of sharply.

"Well, is anyone going to ask him?"

"You know, I heard that Darcy was thinking about it," Stephanie confessed.

"Darcy!?" Quinn exclaimed, not able to help herself. Then thinking that someone might find her reaction weird, she got really interested in the small red writing on her milk carton.

Luckily, the lunch bell rang, and Quinn was saved from any possible questions. Everyone agreed to meet after school for their first practice. Quinn had spoken to the coach earlier that day, and she had agreed to work with them for one more week—if they got the headmistress's permission first. Quinn was headed for Mrs. Hartman's office right now. She wasn't looking forward to it, but she knew she had to talk to her. Earlier that year, she had started an underground newspaper without telling Heartburn, as the girls called Mrs. Hartman, and she had gotten a record detention sentence for it.

Nicole and Esme were waiting for Alicia and Quinn after practice that day. Alicia and Quinn walked out as if they were in a lot of pain.

"You guys look like you just got off a horse after a six-hour ride, or something," Nicole observed as they headed for their bikes.

"Oh, my gosh!" Alicia exclaimed. "I thought I was sore last week after the game, but that was nothing compared to this!"

"Really!" Quinn agreed. "Mrs. Hartman gave her permission to coach us, not to kill us! I don't think Coach Larsen worked us this hard all season. I wonder what's up."

"I heard that the coach of G. Adams called her up to talk about the game, and he said some things about women in sports that made her mad . . ." Nicole said.

"There's the Source at work again," Alicia teased. "You always know everything. How do you hear this stuff, anyway?"

Nicole blushed as she unlocked her bike. She threw her books in the basket and hopped on. The others followed.

"Guys, can we go really slow?" Quinn asked, in a totally pathetic voice. "I'm about to die."

"Wow!" Esme exclaimed, impressed. "If *you* don't want to race to my house, you must be tired!"

Pedaling slowly, the girls reached Esme's without too much conversation. They were going to study for their history test the next day. What with all this soccer stuff, Alicia and Quinn had almost forgotten about it. Luckily, Nicole reminded them, and arranged a study session.

Alicia and Quinn plopped down on Esme's bed, as Nicole pulled out her books, and Esme went downstairs for food.

"I'm never moving," Alicia announced. "I will lie here on Esme's bed forever. I will not move again."

Quinn chuckled. Esme came back into the room with a pitcher of lemonade and two big bags of cookies and chips, and they settled down to study. After about an hour of quizzing each other, Esme called for a break.

"Ugh! These dates and names are spinning around in my head. I can't even remember what century we're in!" she exclaimed. "Can we please take a few minutes off?"

Alicia and Quinn sighed and shut their books. "Sure, Es. I could get into that," Quinn agreed.

"Well, we really have a lot more to cover," Nicole began. Everyone groaned. "But, what's a few minutes. I'm getting kind of sick of this, too."

Esme pulled out her new teen magazine and started leafing through it. Nicole got up and helped herself to another glass of lemonade and a handful of chips.

"Could you toss me those chips, Nicole," Alicia pleaded from the bed. She still hadn't moved since she had plopped down there.

"Of course," Nicole answered, throwing the bag at Alicia. "I would hate to make you move."

"Well, in that case," Alicia began, dark eyes sparkling. "Maybe you'd like to pour me a glass of lemonade, too."

Nicole pretended to bow in front of Alicia. "Anything for the queen."

"Hey, guys!" Esme exclaimed. "Listen to this."

"What now?" Quinn asked, feigning impatience.

"This article on FIRST DATES," Esme answered, as she started to read from the magazine.

The others groaned. Esme was always taking

whatever she read in these magazines so seriously.

"There's a list here of DO's and DON'Ts. I think we should all hear this, especially with this dance coming up."

"You mean, you should follow a list when you go out on a date?" Nicole asked in confusion. This boy-girl stuff was too much to figure out most of the time. Nicole thought she would stick with horses for a while.

"Right," Esme continued. "Here are the DOs:
"1. Get him to talk about himself.
 2. Smile a lot.
 3. Make eye contact.
 4. Positive body language. Touch him frequently when you're making a point.
 5. Laugh at his jokes, even if they're not funny.
 6. Act interested in what he's saying, even if it's boring. Guys love to be the center of attention.
 7. Compliment him on what he's wearing.
 8. Act calm, even if you're not.

"And here are the DON'Ts:
"1. Don't let the conversation lag.
 2. Don't order pizza, spaghetti, French onion soup, artichokes, lobster, or anything you have to eat with chopsticks.
 3. Don't talk too much; let him monopolize the conversation.
 4. If you go bowling, or something, don't beat him. Guys hate to be shown up, especially if it's something they think they're good at.
 5. Don't talk about your ex-boyfriends or his ex-girlfriends.

6. Don't eat too much, but don't eat too little.
7. Don't look as if you spent all afternoon getting ready for this date.
8. When he asks you out, don't say yes too quickly. Act as if your schedule is very busy. Keep him guessing."

The girls all looked at each other for a moment. They didn't know quite what to make of what they'd just heard.

"Is this information supposed to be important for our futures?" Quinn asked. "It sounds totally *degrading* to me. I mean, why *should* I let a guy win, or let him monopolize the conversation! I can't believe you, Es. Why do you need this stuff?"

"Well, if you plan to date," Esme answered, "it's really important to know these things."

"You really take these things seriously?" Quinn asked, serious herself.

"Sure, don't you?" Esme retorted.

"Well, I don't know. I never really thought about it," Quinn answered, suddenly confused. "I mean, why do you need a list of things to do or not do? Why can't you just be yourself?"

Alicia laughed. "*You* would anyway, Quinn."

"So?" Quinn asked, belligerently. "Why would you want to act like you're someone else, or something you're not? Especially if it means being subservient to some guy!"

"It's not that, Quinn," Esme explained, patiently, not really knowing what subservient meant. "It's just that there are right things to do on a date with a boy, and wrong things. We just have to make sure we know them before we start dating."

"Right," Alicia agreed, rolling over onto her back

and hanging her head over the side of the bed.

"I think it's a total waste of time," Nicole put in, opening up her book again. "Don't you, Quinn?"

"I . . . I . . . I guess so," Quinn said uncertainly. She thought there must be a lot more to this dating thing than met the eye. It seemed at first as if it might be pretty easy, but suddenly it sounded really complicated.

Nicole looked at Quinn strangely, but Esme cut her off before she had a chance to say anything.

"Hey, there's a big article in here about the National Cheerleading Contest!" she exclaimed. "These girls look really cool. I wish we had cheerleaders!"

"Who would they cheer?" Alicia asked. "It's not like we have a football team, or anything like that."

"Yeah . . ." Esme began, smiling, "but we do have a State Champion soccer team that has one of its biggest games this weekend. I'd say that'd be something to cheer about."

"That's a great idea!" Alicia exclaimed. "I'd love to do it, too. It's too bad I'll be playing."

"Well, it's not like I wouldn't get anyone else to do it. I bet a lot of girls would want to be cheerleaders," Esme said, sitting up straighter and looking enthusiastic.

"That's true," Quinn said. "I've heard a lot of people say they wished we had cheerleaders at PBP. And it would really help the team. We'd really show those guys then. What do you think, Nicole?"

"I think it's a good idea, too," Nicole replied. "Esme, it would be a perfect thing for you to do. I hate to break this up, but we should get back to studying, I have to be home for dinner soon."

The girls groaned, but one look at the clock reminded them just how late it was. Quinn sighed and opened her book again, knowing that it would be hard to study with all these things to think about—cheerleaders, first dates, the soccer game, and Jonathan. It was going to be a long week.

CHAPTER 4

"What's the big hurry?" Alicia yelled as Quinn raced past her toward the locker room. They had just finished another killer soccer workout, and Alicia wondered how Quinn even had the energy to walk, let alone sprint! Alicia, Nicole, and Esme were strolling slowly across the field, talking about how it had gone.

"Where are you going?" Esme added as Quinn slowed down ahead of them. They walked a little faster to catch up with her.

"Uh . . . uh . . ." Quinn mumbled evasively. "I've . . . uh . . . got some things to do."

"But Quinn," Nicole exclaimed, "I thought everyone was coming to my house and we were all going to switch lab books and compare notes for the science test on Friday." She looked seriously at

34

Quinn, her high brown ponytail swinging neatly from side to side as she walked. Even after a hard workout with the equestrian team, Nicole didn't have a hair out of place. It never ceased to amaze her friends.

"Sorry, Nicole," Quinn replied quickly. "I forgot. Can't we do it tomorrow? We still have a few days."

"I guess so," Nicole answered slowly, turning to Alicia and Esme, who also looked puzzled.

"What do you have to do?" Esme asked directly. She always said what she thought, often without thinking first. "Maybe we can help," she continued, her big light blue eyes looking into Quinn's darker blue ones with concern.

"Thanks, but no thanks, Cornflake," Quinn replied. "I think I can handle it on my own. Maybe I'll bring my science notes over later if I'm done early," she called over her shoulder. Then she sprinted through the double doors leading into the gym.

"That was weird," Alicia commented a few moments later, standing in front of her locker pulling out her books. "I wonder what she's being so mysterious about."

"You know how Quinn is," Esme replied. "It's just one of her moods." Quinn was the newest addition to their group and although they'd been best friends with her for a while, she never ceased to surprise them. Her moods went from great to terrible within seconds. She was definitely the kind of person who took everything in life very much to heart.

"She's probably just busy," Nicole added as she waited for Alicia to change out of her practice clothes and back into her uniform.

"So maybe she'll come by later after she does whatever it is that she's doing," Alicia said, as she zipped up her fuchsia and yellow knapsack and reclipped her black curly hair. "You know how much she loves being mysterious."

"That's true," Esme agreed. "Maybe she's meeting someone . . . like some guy."

"Esme Farrell," Nicole replied with a laugh. "All you think about are guys, guys, guys."

"Really," echoed Alicia. "There's more to life than guys, right?"

"Definitely," Nicole replied. "And we all know that Tyler Stein means nothing to you, Lish."

"Nicole," Alicia admonished, throwing one of her muddy soccer cleats in Nicole's direction. "Stop it!"

"Alicia and Tyler sitting in a tree, k-i-s-s-i-n-g," Esme began, but was cut off by Alicia, who had grabbed her around the waist and was attempting to tickle the life out of her. Within seconds, they were laughing so hard that they'd collapsed into a heap on the locker room floor.

Quinn felt a little bad about lying to her friends, although she wasn't exactly lying. She just wasn't telling them the whole truth. If that counted as a lie, then it was very definitely a white lie. White lies were okay in Quinn's book. They were what made life interesting—especially if you wanted to be a writer.

She pedaled as hard as she could. Flying along the road to Grant Beach, her hair blowing in the wind, she felt so free. But today, not even the beautiful scenery and the thrill of speed made her feel better.

She was in the worst of moods. The most awful part about the whole thing was that she didn't understand what was bothering her.

That was why she'd decided to go to the beach. It was her favorite place to think. She chained her ten-speed to one of the bike racks in the parking lot and walked across the sand to the ocean. The beach was almost empty at this time of day and that suited Quinn just fine.

Quinn marched down to the water's edge and plopped down on the sand. She watched the waves break against the shore and squinted her eyes in the sun to look for any fishing boats on the horizon. That was one of her little brother's favorite things—fishing. He kept saying he wanted to be a fisherman when he grew up. The only problem was that he had a toy fishing rod and he didn't really know how to cast properly. Usually the plastic hook on the end of the pole wound up in someone's hair—like Quinn's. She laughed thinking about it.

Families were very important to Quinn. Hers was very close and they confided in each other most of the time. That was one thing she really couldn't understand about Nicole—and Jonathan. At the thought of Jonathan Stanton, Quinn's stomach started doing flip-flops. And she used to make fun of Esme and all her crushes . . . not that Quinn thought she had a *crush* on Jonathan Stanton—that jerk. But she had to admit that whatever it was she felt about him, she'd never felt about anybody else before.

Quinn picked up a rock and threw it into the water. She didn't understand herself. One minute she wanted to eradicate Jonathan from the face of the earth and the other she started imagining what it would be like to kiss him. Well, maybe not to actually *kiss* him, but she'd like to be his friend or something.

Quinn stood up, kicked off her shoes, and pulled off her socks. She started running along the shore, the water splashing her legs as she jumped the waves. She loved running on the beach. She and Sean used to always race each other when they were younger. She started to feel better, although she wasn't sure why.

But she still didn't know what to do about Jonathan. That article Esme had read said not to beat him at his own game. But that was a real problem, assuming that Quinn did like Jonathan. She was the one who had challenged him to the big soccer game in the first place. Now everybody at PBP was involved and they really wanted to win. She couldn't let them down—at least she didn't think so.

Quinn slackened her pace and stood looking out at the water. The real problem was that sometimes Jonathan could be such a dweeb. More often than not, actually. Like at the pool the other day, when he had that macho attitude about men being better and stronger than women. Women's equality was something Quinn took very seriously. She'd always believed that girls can do anything that guys can do—and better, too. At least that was what her mother had been telling her since she was five. Once her brother Sean had said that she could never be an astronaut because only *men* were allowed to fly in spaceships. They'd started yelling about it and their mother had come in to see what the racket was about. She'd made them laugh by telling Sean that if his little sister went up in a rocket someday it wouldn't surprise her one bit!

So why did she get butterflies in her stomach when she saw Jonathan? There was definitely something about him. For one thing, he stood up for what he wanted. Quinn admired that quality in other people.

Picking up her sandy shoes and socks, Quinn decided that she wasn't going to worry about the Jonathan thing anymore. She was just going to go home, do her homework and forget about him. Then she changed her mind again. After checking her watch, she realized that she had just enough time if she really hurried to catch Esme, Alicia, and Nicole at Nicole's where they were supposed to be studying for the science test.

Quinn hopped on her bike and began pedaling like crazy. She loved biking barefoot, no matter how many times her father told her it was dangerous. She loved the feeling of her bare feet against the pedals and she could always get a better grip that way. Actually, she sometimes wished that she could run track barefoot like that South African girl she'd read about in some running magazine. But she didn't think Mr. Holmes, her track coach, would let her.

Racing through the beautiful streets of Nicole's neighborhood, Quinn couldn't help admiring the perfectly groomed lawns and huge mansions. It amazed her that people actually lived there in these storybook houses, but Nicole was a perfect example. And she was totally normal and nice and not at all affected by all the wealth around her. She'd proven to Quinn that rich people are not necessarily any different than middle-class or poor people, despite the snobby attitudes of some of the girls and teachers at Palm Beach Prep.

Deep in thought, Quinn rode quickly down the Whitcombs' driveway. She almost fell off her bike when she spotted Jonathan leaning against the front door, talking to Adrian Randolph, his best friend from G. Adams. She felt like turning around and going back the way she'd come, but it was too late—they'd already spotted her.

"So, McNair, what's happening?" Jonathan asked in the sarcastic spoiled-brat voice Quinn hated.

"Not much, Stanton," Quinn replied as cooly as possible, trying her hardest to keep the tremor out of her voice.

"Looks like you've been practicing, huh? Putting in as much work as possible before we blow you out of the water next week," he continued in the same tone.

"Get a life, jerk-face!" Quinn blurted out before she could stop herself. Looking down at her outfit, she started to blush. She was such a mess, with her salt-streaked legs and her muddy soccer clothes. And her hair was a total wreck. The whole situation started making her mad. Why should she care how she looked? She never had before—not like this, anyway. "We're going to beat you so badly, you won't know what hit you!" she finally exclaimed.

"Whoooo," Jonathan whistled while Adrian laughed. "We're like really scared."

"Give me a break," Quinn yelled, as she parked her bike and grabbed her knapsack. "I don't have time for this. I'm supposed to meet Nicole."

Quinn stormed off around the corner of the house to use the side entrance that led to Nicole's bedroom.

"You're out of luck, McNair," Jonathan said from right behind her. Quinn jumped in surprise. "Nicole went out to dinner with her grandparents," he explained.

Quinn whirled around to face him. It hadn't even occurred to her that neither Alicia's nor Esme's bikes were there. "Oh," she replied casually, blushing again from head to toe. "No problem. I'll just talk to her later."

"Should I tell her to call you?" Jonathan asked.

"Don't bother," Quinn replied quickly. "I don't need you to do me any favors. Where'd your sidekick run off to anyway?" she added, because she hadn't seen Adrian leave.

"Whoa," Jonathan exclaimed. "You are one tough cookie, McNair. Adrian had to go home. Why do you care?"

"I don't. Just leave me alone, okay," Quinn mumbled as she rounded the corner to get her bike. Her eyes had misted over with the start of a couple of tears and there was no way she was going to let Jonathan know that he had gotten to her. She had to get out of there—fast.

"So . . . uh . . . Quinn . . ." Jonathan began. "About the . . . uh, game . . . I . . . uh . . . I wondered whether maybe we should . . . uh . . . get together at some point to . . . uh . . . discuss the . . . uh . . . situation a little . . ."

Quinn could not get over the change in Jonathan. One minute he was the cockiest jerk and then the next he was acting like a human being. She could not figure him out one bit. Was it because Adrian had left, and he didn't have to show off anymore?

"Uh . . . sure," Quinn muttered in reply. "Like, when were you thinking of?"

"Uh . . . soon . . . I guess. What about tonight?" Jonathan blurted out.

"Okay," Quinn agreed without thinking. Then she thought that she had accepted too quickly. After all, the article Esme had read said that girls should play a little hard to get.

"You want to do it over pizza maybe 'cause I'm sort of hungry. I don't know about you . . ." Jonathan's voice trailed off.

In her daze it suddenly occurred to Quinn that Jonathan Stanton, Mr. Cool, was nervous. And he was nervous because of her. That was a weird feeling. Quinn didn't know how she felt about it. "Yeah, I could eat, I guess," she finally replied, avoiding looking directly into his eyes.

"Do you want to go now?" he asked.

"Yeah, I guess," Quinn said quickly. "But I better call home first."

Quinn followed Jonathan into the house and headed for the phone in the kitchen. Jonathan told her he had to get something, but he'd be back in a minute. She stood still for a second trying to digest the fact that Jonathan Stanton had actually asked her out on a date, that magical four-letter word. She was about to go on her first date. Maybe it was a good thing that Esme had read her that article. Quinn shook her head in surprise, and shrugging, picked up the phone.

CHAPTER 5

Quinn and Jonathan didn't talk much on their way to Pizzarama. It would have been difficult anyway since Quinn was riding her bike and Jonathan was skateboarding. Quinn couldn't help herself. She kept sneaking peeks in Jonathan's direction. He was a great skateboarder, that was for sure. He also happened to be looking pretty good in his hightops and ripped jeans.

Pizzarama was hopping as usual. Quinn kept praying that she wouldn't see anyone she knew. At the same time, she kind of wanted everybody to know about her big date. Meanwhile, Jonathan hadn't said more than a few words since they'd left the house. Quinn started worrying that he was probably sorry he'd asked her in the first place. Then she started thinking of possible ways to leave that wouldn't be too embarrassing for either of them. But nothing came to mind and the whole situation left her tongue-tied.

"So," Jonathan began, as he jabbed at the ice in his Coke with his straw, keeping his eyes riveted on the glass in front of him. "What do you like on your pizza?"

Quinn took a sip of her soda. She had to think for a minute. She was having two problems. First, she was so nervous that she felt as if she'd never be hungry again. Second, she liked disgusting stuff on her pizza. Then there was the issue of the pizza itself. The article had said that pizza ranked up there with spaghetti as a definite no-no for a first-date food.

"Quinn," Jonathan prodded her, finally bringing her back to the present. "You did want pizza, didn't you?"

"Yeah," Quinn replied. "Plain is fine with me, you know, with just your basic cheese and tomato. I don't usually go for all that other stuff."

"Oh," Jonathan said, disappointment in his voice. "I know it's disgusting, but I love all that stuff. Sometimes I even order anchovies." He laughed, his brown eyes twinkling. "But that's okay, if you don't want it, you know."

"Okay," Quinn agreed quickly. Great, so now she was being forced to eat the number-one bad date food and she couldn't even have it the way she liked it because she was trying to be a good date. This dating stuff was really complicated. The whole experience was making her sweat.

After they'd ordered, they both sat there, looking down at the table. "So," Quinn began, determined not to let the conversation lag. Of course, she would have to be careful not to talk too much. There seemed to be such a fine line between the DOs and the DON'Ts. "When did you start skateboarding?" she asked. That was a good question, she thought. Get him talking about himself.

"A long time ago," Jonathan said proudly. "In New York practically everybody skateboards, especially if you live in the city."

"Oh," Quinn replied. So far so good, she thought, but what should she say next? "I ride my brother's old one once in a while, but I'm not good yet or anything. Actually, the wheels are kind of loose and rusted."

"That's not good at all. It's really important to have at least a decent board or you don't give yourself a chance," Jonathan explained.

"Oh," Quinn replied. Great. She must sound like some sort of big-time airhead the way she kept saying "oh." What was with her? She never had this much trouble talking.

"Do you want to maybe try my skateboard?" Jonathan asked. "The parking lot out back is great. There's hardly any bumps or potholes. And there's this great little ramp that they use for deliveries. We could go out there after we eat."

"Okay," Quinn agreed.

"Hey, you better have some of this pizza," Jonathan said, picking up a gooey slice and putting it on a plate for her. "I've been known to inhale an entire pie in minutes."

"My brothers and I once finished off four pies in half an hour," Quinn said, laughing. "I'm sure it was a Pizzarama record!" Oh, no, she thought, suddenly. Now he'll think that I eat too much.

"Uh oh," Jonathan joked. "I better be careful then. Or next thing I know you'll challenge me to a pizza-eating contest."

Quinn took a deep breath and tried to relax. That article said to act calm even if you weren't. It wasn't exactly easy to *feel* calm with Jonathan sitting right across the table from her. After a few more minutes, though, she was surprised at how much fun she was having. She'd hardly even worried about the actual mechanics of eating pizza. She had to try really hard not to crack up, though, or a glob of cheese might come shooting out of her mouth. Other than that one basic problem, she was doing okay.

"Speaking of contests," she said, after swallowing what felt like a huge mouthful of cheese and crust, "we should probably talk about the game."

"Good idea," Jonathan agreed, pulling a third piece of pizza onto his plate.

"We were talking at lunch, and we decided that because *we* challenged *you*, then we should play at PBP."

"Uh uh," Jonathan said fiercely through a mouthful, shaking his head. "The guys definitely want to play at G. Adams. See, since *you* challenged *us*, we're supposed to get the home field advantage. That's the way they do it in professional sports, so I rest my case."

"I know all about professional sports," Quinn said defensively. She couldn't help the sarcasm in her voice. Jonathan was being so condescending.

"Well, maybe the rules are different for girls,"

Jonathan continued. "But we follow the official rules pretty closely and that's the way they do it."

"So do we," Quinn countered. She took a long drink of Coke, hoping it would cool the tops of her ears. Her temper was very definitely rising. She couldn't believe Jonathan was starting this stupid attitude all over again.

"I don't know how you can," Jonathan continued in the same obnoxious tone, "since there aren't any professional women's sports."

"Yeah, right, like that's a fact, Mr. Know-It-All." The soda had definitely not worked at all. Quinn felt like killing Jonathan. His stupid macho attitude was back in full force.

"It *is* a fact," Jonathan went on. "Women's sports just aren't exciting. No one really cares about them."

"Maybe it's because they haven't been given a chance. Anyway, what about professional women's tennis, and skiing, and horse racing," Quinn said loudly. "Some of the best jockeys in the country are women. And how about the Olympics? I suppose people only watch when *men* break world records!" Quinn fumed, her voice dripping with sarcasm.

"Chill out," Jonathan shot back. Some of the other people in the restaurant had started to look their way. "I don't know what's with you. You take everything so seriously."

Quinn felt as if her body were on fire. "Jonathan Stanton," she screamed, "you are without a doubt the biggest jerk in the entire world and also the world's stupidest male chauvinist!"

She slid out of the booth as fast as she could.

Unfortunately, in her hurry, she knocked the rest of the pizza off the table and into Jonathan's lap. The kids at the table across from them started to laugh and point. And Jonathan looked like he wished he had a gun. Tomato sauce and cheese were splattered across his white T-shirt. Of course, Quinn didn't know that he had been thinking of apologizing, but now that was out of the question.

Quinn biked home in a haze of anger. She wanted to murder Jonathan. She could not believe the way he had acted. How she could have thought for even the tiniest second that she liked him was beyond her. He was the most disgusting, unlikable, totally hateable creep with a capital C in the entire universe. Uuugghh!

Quinn popped a wheelie into her driveway and almost crashed as she tried to avoid one of Patrick's Tonka trucks which was lying by the side of the driveway. Pat was such a brat! He always left his stuff lying everywhere. In her rage, Quinn stormed up the back steps and tripped over one of her middle brother Brian's whiffle ball bats. Brothers were such pains. Boys in general were total jerks and Quinn was really sick of them.

By the time she'd made it into the kitchen, she felt as if murder would be too good a fate for Jonathan. She remembered one of Alicia's favorite horror movies in which the victim had toothpicks stuck slowly up his fingernails until he confessed. That might be just the thing for Jonathan. It was pretty gross actually.

Quinn opened the fridge to find something to eat. It was definitely time for someone to go food shopping. She forgot whose turn it was. They usually rotated in groups of two. They got the best stuff when it was Quinn and Sean because they loaded up on potato chips and cookies and stuff. Quinn found a plastic food container and pulled it out to examine its contents.

"Hey, Quinno, what's up?" Sean said loudly, interrupting her train of thought.

"Nothing at all," Quinn replied grumpily.

"I see you've got your heart set on having some of my famous tuna surprise," Sean kidded her, pointing to the container on the counter.

"Yuck!" Quinn retorted, recoiling from the container as if she'd been stung. "You know how much I hate hot tuna. Tuna was not invented to be cooked. It's totally unnatural."

"Please," Sean implored. "Spare me your food fetishes. Anyway, I thought you just went out to dinner."

Quinn blushed. She couldn't help it. Just thinking about her date with Jonathan made her crazy. "Yeah . . . I . . . uh . . . I did . . . but I'm like really hungry anyway . . . you know how like if you have like Chinese food sometimes you're like really hungry even after you just ate. It's this like chemical thing I forget but—"

"Quinn Mary Margaret McNair," Sean interrupted. "Stop babbling. All I did was ask if you were hungry—I didn't expect to be given a bio lecture about food groups or whatever it is you're talking about."

"Leave me alone. Just get out of here, okay," Quinn sputtered. Her face was bright red and a few tears glistened on her eyelashes. She couldn't believe she was crying. And it was all Jonathan's fault. She stormed out of the kitchen, slamming the door on her way. Quinn loved slamming doors when she was mad. She used to do it a lot when she was younger, but now that she was almost a teenager she had pretty much broken the habit. Except for moments like these.

She slammed the door to her room really hard. One of her favorite framed posters, Maurice Sendak's *Wild Things*, fell down and hit the floor with a loud thump. Quinn threw herself facedown on her bed and pulled her pillow over her head. And then she started to cry. What was it with her? Why couldn't she be like other people and not get so upset about things? And why did she care what stupid Jonathan Stanton thought about anything? He was a total loser and a jerk and she hated his guts and hoped she never saw him ever again. But, of course she'd have to see him again, and soon, because of the soccer challenge and everything. And that was all her fault, too. Why was she always opening her big mouth?

Suddenly, she felt someone sit down on her bottom—someone kind of heavy. "Get off me, Sean," Quinn barked, pulling the pillow off her head and glaring at him.

"Now that I finally have your attention, Quinnster, would you like to tell me what's going on?"

"Nothing is going on, Sean. Stop being such a dork!" Quinn yelled, pulling the pillow over her head again.

"Quinnster," Sean urged gently. "You know you

can talk to me. And I bet whatever it is really isn't all that bad," he continued reassuringly. "But first let me tell you my news. Get out from under that pillow. You're going to freak."

Quinn debated with herself. Half of her felt more than justified in lying there feeling sorry for herself. But the other half was curious about whatever it was that Sean was about to tell her. The other half won. She sat up, put the tear-soaked pillow behind her head and composed her features into what she hoped was a calm expression. She folded her hands on her lap and nodded at Sean.

"Your majesty," Sean began kidding around, "now that I have your royal attention, I would just like to tell you that the Nueva Beat is about to do a demo tape."

"No way!" Quinn exclaimed in shock, as she jumped up and down on the bed. "That's fantastic!"

"Thanks," Sean said modestly. "Now it's just one song, but still—"

"That's still great!" Quinn exclaimed, reaching out to hug her brother. "I always knew you could do it. I'm telling you, the Fine Young Cannibals better watch out for you and Ricky."

"I wish," Sean replied with a smile. "Anyway, I just wanted you to know that. You can come to the studio when we do it maybe if you want. It'll probably be pretty cool."

"Really," Quinn echoed, smiling broadly. Her brother was the greatest. She shouldn't be so obnoxious to him, even if it was hard sometimes. At least, he had made her forget about the Jonathan situation for a while.

"Earth to Quinn," Sean cut into her thoughts. "What's happening in the devious mind of the young Quinnster McNair?"

Quinn giggled. Maybe she should ask Sean about the Jonathan thing. Not directly. She would just change the names to protect the innocent. That way no harm would be done.

"Sean," Quinn began tentatively, "I kind of wanted to ask you something, if you have a minute that is."

"Shoot," Sean answered quickly, as he lay down on her bed with his head hanging over the side.

"Well, I have this friend," Quinn said.

"Who?" Sean asked immediately. "I know all your friends."

"Sean, you don't know her and anyway that's not the point. I swore that I wouldn't tell anybody what she said so I can't tell you her name."

"Okay, okay. I didn't realize we were in the middle of an episode of *21 Jump Street*."

"Don't make fun of me, Sean. This is serious."

Sean looked at her, with the most serious face he could muster.

"Anyway," Quinn continued slowly, "she kind of likes this guy and he's playing in the soccer challenge against us, and she kind of doesn't know what to do about winning because she's sort of afraid . . ." Quinn paused and tugged on a clump of her thick, red hair. "Well, maybe not *afraid*, but worried that if she wins, he won't, like, be her friend and stuff . . . because guys supposedly really hate to be beaten," she finished quickly, looking at Sean.

"Hmmm," Sean murmured, as he pulled himself

up to a sitting position on the bed. "It is certainly a fact that the male ego is incredibly huge, and that winning is a big deal."

"Yeah," Quinn said.

"But it's also true that everybody's got to do what they have to do, you know what I mean?" Sean asked with a wink.

Quinn laughed. "Maybe," she replied.

"Well," Sean said, "I hope that helps your . . . um . . . friend, a little."

"Oh, it will, it will," Quinn said quickly.

"Is there anything else I can do for you?" Sean asked. "If not, then I must go hit the books."

"That's okay, Sean. I think I'm going to go to bed. It's been a long day."

After Sean left her room, Quinn lay there thinking about things. She didn't understand, she just didn't, and nothing made sense the way it used to before she'd met Jonathan. Going to PBP at the beginning of the year had been hard, probably the hardest thing Quinn had ever had to do. But this thing with Jonathan seemed so much worse. Maybe because it made so little sense. And she couldn't talk to any of her friends about it. She still didn't know what to do about the game, even after what Sean said. She wasn't about to throw a big soccer match just to get a guy, especially if she was still mad at him.

In the midst of this complicated train of thought, Quinn fell asleep, still wearing her muddy soccer clothes.

CHAPTER
6

It was fourth period study hall and Esme and Alicia were supposed to be putting the finishing touches on their English homework. It was one of Mr. Holmes's assignments, and Alicia was really into it. They had to look at a photograph and explain what they thought was happening in it. Alicia had found an old picture of her great-grandmother as a little girl posing in an old-fashioned dress with a high collar and everything. There was a window behind her and Alicia had the definite feeling that all her great-grandmother wanted was to be able to go outside and play. She looked so uncomfortable and trapped. So, Alicia was trying to write about those feelings.

She was chewing on the end of her pencil, deep in thought, when she was jolted back to reality by

Esme, who bumped into her by mistake, knocking her elbow off the table.

"What are you doing?" Alicia hissed at Esme.

"I'm cheerleading. I didn't mean to hit you," Esme huffed, taking one look at Alicia's miffed expression.

"Es, you are totally crazy," Alicia whispered. "How can you cheerlead by yourself, sitting down?"

"Watch me," Esme replied, a determined expression on her face. "B-E, A-G-G, R-E-S-S, I-V-E," Esme began, gesturing madly from side to side and waving her arms.

"Shh," Alicia admonished her with a frown. "Mrs. Finn will kill us."

"Let me finish," Esme whispered back. "BE AGGRESSIVE!" she said loudly as she thrust her arms up in the air. The momentum caused her to tip backwards and she landed with a loud crash, her legs sticking up in the air.

Alicia began to giggle hysterically, covering her mouth to hold in her laughter. So did most of the other girls in study hall, especially Cara Knowles and Jesse Langdon.

"Esme Farrell," Mrs. Finn intoned from the front desk. "Come up here, please. Immediately."

"Yes, ma'am," Esme mumbled from her position on the floor.

She slowly picked herself up, left the table, and marched to the front of the room, her head held high.

At lunch later that morning, Esme was still acting annoyed about the whole study hall fiasco.

"Es, will you chill out," Alicia said directly. "It was pretty funny, you know."

"And you didn't even really get in trouble," Nicole commented practically. "Considering it was Finn and everything."

"Really," echoed Quinn. "Anyway, I love the whole idea of you cheerleading in your chair—kind of like being a couch cheerleader, you know, instead of a couch potato."

Alicia and Nicole giggled.

"That's not funny," Esme whined. "I don't want to talk about it anymore."

"Okay," Nicole agreed quickly. "So let's hear some of your cheers."

Esme's face lit up. "One sec," she said, as she began to rummage through some loose papers stuck in one of her notebooks.

"How about this," Quinn cut in. When it came to rhymes and making things up, she just couldn't help herself. She loved putting words together.

Everyone looked at her expectantly, including Esme.

"GA take a hike, PBP's about to strike!" Quinn said loudly.

"I don't know, Q," Esme commented bluntly. "It doesn't exactly make sense and what would the moves be? I've got this great idea for a human pyramid and all kinds of round-offs and split-jumps," Esme continued breathlessly, still frantically searching through her papers.

"Be patient for a minute, Es," Quinn said, biting her lip as she tried to think up more cheers. "Genius takes time. Here's another one," she said with a smile. "Watch out GA, PBP's going to blow you away!"

Nicole and Alicia laughed. Esme looked expectantly at Quinn.

"Well, ex-cuse me, Esme Farrell," Quinn said seriously, trying to pretend she was hurt that nobody had liked her cheers. "Let's hear some of yours, then, since you're obviously less than thrilled with mine," she finished with a giggle. "I may never write again," she added, pretending to look extremely upset.

"Here it is!" Esme exclaimed, clutching a piece of rumpled notebook paper and letting out a huge sigh of relief. "I made up two versions so you guys tell me which one you like better." She cleared her throat. "Roses are red, violets are blue, G. Adams' gonna lose, boo hoo hoo!"

Nicole, Alicia, and Quinn looked at each other and didn't say anything. "Let's hear the next one," Alicia said tactfully.

Esme cleared her throat again. "Roses are red, violets are blue, PBP's all set to, beat the pants off of you!"

"Es," Quinn said quietly, "after lunch maybe you should show us some of the routines you're thinking of. Then maybe the words will just sort of fall into place."

"Maybe," Esme agreed with a smile. "That's a really really good idea, Quinn."

Just then Cara came sweeping by with Jesse and Patty. "Great going in study hall, Esme," she said obnoxiously, flicking her smooth golden-blonde hair from one shoulder to the other as she spoke.

"Really," echoed Jesse, her most loyal sidekick.

"Shut up, Cara," Alicia cut in. Cara drove Alicia completely up the wall.

"Yeah," agreed Esme. "You probably wouldn't know a cheerleader if you fell over one."

"What does cheerleading have to do with anything?" Patty asked, unable to contain the curiosity in her voice.

Cara gave her an icy glare.

"Not that we care," Jesse said.

"Esme's starting a cheerleading squad for the big soccer game," Quinn stated proudly. "And she's figured out some terrific routines."

"Yeah," echoed Nicole and Alicia from their positions on either side of Esme.

"So let's see one of your cheers," Jesse prodded.

"I don't know," Esme began hesitantly. "I don't think there's enough room here, you know."

"You're just scared, Esme," Cara challenged. "Because you know you're no good."

"Get a grip, Knowles," Quinn cut in. "You have no clue what you're talking about, as usual."

All the commotion had caught the attention of some of the other girls in the lunchroom.

"What's going on?" Stephanie asked from a few tables away.

"Esme's going to start a cheerleading squad," Quinn yelled back.

"I'd love to be a cheerleader," Anne Marie Hayes called out from across the room.

"You just want to show off in front of Zach Burnett," Missy Madden teased her.

"You're just jealous, Missy," Anne Marie kidded, "because you know you're so uncoordinated that you would probably trip over your own two feet in front of all those people."

"Would not," Missy argued. "If I want to be a cheerleader then I can be one. I'm going to ask Esme."

Before Esme knew what was happening, a group of girls had surrounded her, all babbling excitedly about being cheerleaders.

"Excuse me," Cara cut in loudly, trying to get everyone's attention away from Esme. "But I'm forming my own cheerleading squad."

Esme stared at her, her mouth open in surprise. "But that's not fair—" Esme began.

"Of course it is," Cara cut her off.

"But, we don't need *two* squads to cheer for *one* team," Virginia said practically.

"Who said we were all going to be cheering for the same team?" Cara shot back with a smug expression on her face.

"Just what are you saying, Knowles?" Esme asked directly.

"My squad is going to cheer for the boys," Cara explained patiently, staring right at Esme.

"What!" Stephanie exploded, walking right up to Cara.

"But that's ridiculous," Chelsea commented.

"Really," agreed Quinn. "It's supposed to be the girls against the boys, Cara, remember?"

"So what?" Cara retorted. "I'm sure there's lots of girls who would rather cheer for the G. Adams guys than for the girls."

"You are such a spoilsport," Alicia noted in disgust.

"Shut up, stupid. You're just jealous," Cara shot back.

"Yeah," echoed Jesse. "Because you know you'd never make it on our squad."

"I'm playing in the game, jerk-face," Alicia retorted.

"Big deal," Mimi said, supporting Queen Cara, as usual.

"Whoever wants to be on my squad can meet me after school by the bike racks," Cara said pointedly. "We're going to have a lot more fun, that's for sure," she continued. "And the guys will be so so excited."

With that, she walked away, Jesse, Mimi, and Patty following close behind.

Esme stood where she was, clenching and unclenching her fists.

"Don't worry, Es," Alicia consoled her.

"Our squad will be so much better," Anne Marie and Missy said.

"Hey, Nicole, when should we have the first meeting of our squad?" Esme asked.

"Our squad?" Nicole said in surprise. "I'm not on the squad."

"Oh, yes you are," Esme insisted. "You're not playing in the game. So of course you have to be on the squad."

"It'll be fun, Nicole," Alicia prodded her.

"Yeah," Quinn agreed. "And you know how much we need the support."

"I don't believe this," Nicole mumbled. "I just do not believe this."

"Yes, you do, Nicole," Esme encouraged her. "You'll have a great time. Believe me."

CHAPTER 7

"**E**sme, I wasn't kidding," Nicole said firmly as she slipped out of her uniform skirt and into a pair of baggy gym shorts. She walked over to her perfectly neat and organized closet and hung up the skirt.

"Nicole, I wasn't kidding either," Esme retorted, her jaw set in a firm line. "And I won't take no for an answer."

"Es, it's not your decision, you know," Nicole said. "And I don't see why I have to make a fool out of myself in front of hundreds of people just because you say so."

"Nicole, you are not going to make a fool out of yourself. Anyway, you're used to performing in front of crowds. I mean, you've been riding in horse shows since you could walk practically," Esme concluded as she sat down at Nicole's vanity to braid her hair.

Nicole was standing in the middle of her walk-in closet, lining up the brown loafers she'd worn to school that day next to the black loafers she'd worn the day before. She was very careful about not wearing out her shoes.

"Nicole, did you hear me?" Esme asked insistently.

"Yes, I heard you," Nicole calmly replied as she bent down to tie her sneakers. "Cheerleading has nothing to do with horseback riding. And no I will not, I repeat, will not, be a cheerleader."

"Nicole, I hate to do this to you," Esme began, "but I guess I don't have a choice." She paused dramatically, and swiveled around on the stool where she was sitting to look at Nicole. "Do you realize . . . no, I guess you don't . . ."

"Yeah," Nicole prodded her. "Es, cut the drama, please. What are you talking about?"

"Well, it's not easy to say . . ." Esme let her voice trail off. "But someone's got to tell you—"

"Es, come on. Will you tell me?" Nicole interrupted her.

"All right," Esme replied solemnly. "Nicole, unless you cheerlead for the team, Quinn and Alicia swear they're not going to play."

"Es, stop making me feel guilty."

"Then tell me you'll at least let me show you a few cheers, please," Esme implored.

"I guess," Nicole replied quickly. "Where do you want to do them?"

"Maybe out back by the pool," Esme suggested.

"After a quick snack maybe," she added with a sly giggle.

About twenty cookies later, Esme and Nicole strolled out to the backyard. Esme lay down on the ground. "Oooh," she moaned, "I'm such a beached whale. Why did you let me eat all those cookies?"

"As if anyone can ever stop you from eating anything, Esme Farrell," Nicole said with a smile. "Quinn's so right about you. You are a Hoover."

"Stop that vacuum cleaner stuff," Esme pouted. "It's kind of insulting, you know."

Esme stood up slowly and stretched. "B-E, A-G-G-, R-E-S-S, I-V-E," she yelled. Then she did a pretty well executed round-off. "BE AGGRESSIVE!" she screamed as she did a split jump and threw up her arms.

"Wow," was all Nicole could say.

"Now you try it," Esme suggested breathlessly. "It's really really easy. You'll see."

"I don't think so," Nicole replied quietly. "Remember how bad I was in gymnastics in third grade?"

"You weren't so bad," Esme disagreed. "You always got marks for doing the best headstands and forward rolls."

"I don't think an ability to do headstands will help me much now. Be serious, Es."

"Let's take this step by step. Try a round-off first," Esme instructed patiently. She stood back, hands on her hips, to watch.

Nicole took a deep breath. She stood there without moving.

"What are you, Whitcomb? A lawn ornament or

what?" Jonathan sneered as he skateboarded around the pool and came to a stop right by Nicole and Esme.

"We're cheerleading," Esme said with a giggle. "What did you think we were doing?"

"Not a whole lot," his friend Adrian added.

"Definitely not cheerleading," Jonathan put in, as he skateboarded from side to side.

"I don't know why you're bothering," Adrian said with a smile. "I mean we're going to whip you girls."

"Really," Jonathan echoed obnoxiously. "This game is going to be over before it even begins."

"That's what you think," Nicole said loudly. "You obviously haven't seen us play lately."

"I don't need to see anything to know," Jonathan retorted. "You, a cheerleader," he continued, looking Nicole up and down, a wry smile curling his lips. "This I have got to see."

"What does that mean?" Esme piped up, her cheeks flushing in anger. "Nicole is like one of the best cheerleaders on the entire squad."

"Yeah," Nicole agreed, suddenly turning red as she realized that she'd just admitted, no gloated, about being a cheerleader. Wasn't that exactly what she was arguing with Esme about *not* doing? Things were going from bad to worse so fast it made her head spin. Not to mention that she really thought the whole game thing was getting kind of out of hand. She was sick and tired of arguing with Jonathan about it. At this point, she was beginning not to even care if they won.

The boys walked off, leaving Nicole and Esme alone again.

"So, Nicole," Esme said cheerfully, "let's try that one again, now that you've agreed to be a cheerleader and everything."

Nicole groaned. "I don't believe this . . ." she muttered.

The next day at school, PBP was buzzing with pre-game chatter and endless speculations about the two cheerleading squads. Some of the more boy-crazy girls thought cheering for the boys was a terrific idea, while others thought it was completely ridiculous. Esme suggested silk-screening special T-shirts for her squad, and arranged to make them during their morning study hall.

"I can't wait to see the T-shirts!" Esme exclaimed, later in the day. "Do you want to come with me to the art room to check them out?" she asked Nicole, a wicked gleam in her eye.

"That's right, Nicole," Quinn urged her with a smile. "Now that you're a cheerleader and everything."

"Quinn," Nicole said quietly. "Stop teasing me." She trudged slowly up the stairs behind Esme.

Esme explained to Nicole that Anne Marie had had the brilliant idea of borrowing the field hockey kilts from the team. They were the school colors, green and white, and they were also a cute style and very short. She ran to a table at the back of the art room and let out a gasp.

"No way!" Esme sputtered. "Nicole, come look at this total disaster. Someone ruined our beautiful T-shirts."

The bright green word "girls" on the back of each

T-shirt had been circled in red and then crossed out on every single shirt.

"I don't believe this," Esme continued.

"Who do you think would do this anyway?" Nicole asked.

Just then Ms. Kleber, the art teacher, came walking into the room.

"Ms. Kleber," Esme began, a hysterical note in her voice, "did you see anyone near our T-shirts today? They're totally ruined."

"Ruined?" Ms. Kleber asked, a befuddled expression on her face. She had a reputation for being seriously out-to-lunch—definitely the classic spacey artist type. "I thought they looked very nice, especially after the red was added, you know, for the sake of the composition. And red and green are famous for complementing each other. It's all a question of harmony actually."

Nicole and Esme looked at each other.

"Well, did you see anybody near the shirts recently?" Nicole asked bluntly.

"Oh, yes," Ms. Kleber replied without hesitation. "Cara Knowles and Patty Porter were here right before lunch."

"That little creep!" Esme squealed.

"What?" Ms. Kleber asked, a surprised expression on her face.

"Nothing," Nicole said quickly. "We've got it under control." She nudged Esme, who was about to say something else. "Thank you, Ms. Kleber," Nicole said sweetly.

Suddenly something caught Nicole's eye. Hanging up by the window were the shirts Cara had made for her squad. They looked exactly like the ones Esme had originally made, except that they had the word "boys" on the back instead of "girls." Quickly, Nicole ushered Esme out of the art room.

"What are you doing?" Esme asked.

"Just making sure you don't do anything stupid. Anyway, I have an idea."

"What kind of idea?"

"A great idea to get back at Knowles-It-All," Nicole said quietly, as she proceeded to whisper her plan to Esme.

After school, Nicole, Esme, and Anne Marie, whom they'd recruited to help carry out the plan, sneaked into the art room. Ms. Kleber was not there.

"Let's go for it," Anne Marie said. "Grab that silk screen."

They proceeded to make the same adjustments to the other squad's shirts as Cara had done to theirs, putting a red circle and slash through the word "boys." They had just finished their last shirt when a screech came from the direction of the art room door.

"Get away from there," Cara bellowed as she ran up to Esme.

"We're just trying to make things fair, like you did," Esme retorted.

"I don't know what you're talking about," Cara hissed.

"Why don't you just admit it," Anne Marie prodded her. "We know it was you."

"You're crazy," Cara replied, not looking any of them in the eye.

"Well, I've got the perfect solution to this whole

T-shirt mess," Esme said coolly, glancing at Nicole.
"I think we should all switch shirts."

Cara thought this over for a minute, chewing on
the end of a strand of her blonde hair.

"Under the condition that there will be no more
dirty tricks," Esme added forcefully.

"You're such a genius," Cara said sarcastically.

"Well, I think it's a great idea," Nicole and Anne
Marie enthused, backing her up. "Really, really
great."

The three of them looked at each other and
winked.

CHAPTER
8

"Go, go, go . . ." the entire PBP soccer team was chanting. They were lying down on their stomachs about five feet apart from each other along the edge of the soccer field. The first girl in line had to jump up, run over all the girls in line, and throw herself down five feet from the last girl in line. Meanwhile, the second girl in line was running right behind her. It was Quinn's favorite drill, even if her lungs burned by the time it was over. They had to go five times around the field!

After practice today, the entire team was going over to watch G. Adams practice. Coach Larsen thought it would be a good idea to see what they were up against. As soon as this announcement was made, Quinn started feeling really nervous. She had lost the ball three times during the footwork drill.

She passed the ball to the wrong person during the three-on-two drill, and now she kept forgetting to get up and run when she was the first girl in line. It was becoming a little ridiculous. Quinn would be more than glad when this whole challenge business was over.

Finally, practice was finished, and the team was biking over to G. Adams. Coach Larsen was driving anyone who didn't have a bike. Quinn wished she had told Coach that she had left her bike at home. She felt as if she were pedaling to her doom, or something.

"They look pretty good," Virginia said, sounding a little worried, as the girls approached the main playing field at G. Adams. The boys' soccer team was in the middle of a scrimmage and they were playing with incredible intensity. They definitely were taking this game seriously.

"I had no idea they were so fast," Nina put in, a little awestruck, as the group stopped at the edge of the field.

Alicia laughed, startling everyone.

"What's so funny, Lish? They look totally serious!"

"I know," Alicia began, trying to regain her composure, "that's their problem. They definitely don't look like they have as much fun in practice as we do—and *we* are the State Champs! I wonder what that means?"

Everyone else laughed, breaking the tension. "That's true, Lish," Quinn agreed. "We *must* be doing something right!"

"Girls," Coach Larsen called out, "watch their

center forward—he's the one playing on the red team." Quinn followed the coach's gaze out to the dark-haired center forward. He was fast—very fast. And he had great footwork. Quinn watched as he escaped three almost-certain tackles to set up a barrage of shots on goal. He was really good. Now, on top of her troubles with Jonathan, she started to feel nervous about the game itself.

"Who is that anyway?" Stephanie asked, shielding her eyes from the afternoon sun.

"It's Jonathan Stanton," Darcy answered. "I forgot how cute he was. Oh, look, and did you see that pass Adrian made?"

"Darcy!" Vanessa reprimanded. "We're here to scout for the game, not the dance!" She paused and squinted across the field for a better look. "Though I have to admit, Jonathan definitely is cute!"

Quinn swallowed hard. She wished the middle of the field would open up and pull Jonathan down into the earth. Then all her problems would be solved—except then she might miss him, maybe.

Just then, the G. Adams coach looked their way. He walked over to Coach Larsen. He was a really big guy, or rather, he had a really big stomach. Quinn thought his voice sounded like he had swallowed a megaphone. Then she decided that maybe he was talking so loud just to psyche out the PBP team.

"Well, well," he boomed. "Coach Larsen and the *girls*." Quinn hated the way he said the word "girls," as if they were a lower form of animal or something. Her back stiffened in anger. She had no idea that adult men could act just like Jonathan about girls playing soccer.

"A little nervous about the big game, eh?" the coach continued, glancing around to see if he had the whole PBP team's attention.

How Coach Larsen kept her cool was beyond Quinn. "Haven't you ever heard of scouting, Coach?" she asked in her sweetest voice. "All the professional teams do it, and you know as State Champions we try to conduct ourselves in the most professional manner possible." Quinn loved the way the coach emphasized that they were State Champs. It definitely seemed to do the trick. The G. Adams coach quickly turned and walked away.

"So, girls, check out the guys you'll be playing directly against, and try to observe their style of play. Tomorrow, we'll talk about what kind of defense to use against them," Coach Larsen told the girls.

"And how to score goals, right?" Stephanie asked.

"Oh, as State Champs, I think you guys definitely know how to score goals, but we'll work on some new plays tomorrow," she said and then waved to the girls as she turned to leave.

The girls all spread out to observe the team some more. After about ten minutes, most of them started to drift away.

"Quinn! Earth to Quinn!" Alicia said right in her ear.

Quinn started, and turned toward Alicia.

"That's only about the tenth time I've called you," she complained. "Are you ready to get going now?"

"I think I'll stay a few more minutes to watch," Quinn answered. "You know, since this whole game was my idea, I feel like I have put in some extra effort or something."

"Well, I've got to go. I promised my mom I'd be home early to help her with dinner," Alicia explained. "You'll be home later, right? Give me a call, okay?"

After Alicia took off, Quinn was left by herself. Even Coach Larsen had left. For some strange reason, Quinn was hoping to talk to Jonathan. It would probably be her last chance to speak to him before the game. But, after the scrimmage was over, Jonathan left the field with a bunch of guys without so much as a backward glance.

Quinn went out onto the field after everyone had left. She spent a few minutes just standing there. She really loved soccer. It was too bad that everything was getting so complicated. Her mother said that every year you get older, life gets more and more complicated. Maybe that was what was happening to her.

She walked off the field, dragging her feet. She got on her bike and, pedaling slowly, she headed home, thinking about the game. She was about two blocks away when a loud shout behind her startled her into riding right off the sidewalk.

"Look out!"

Quinn turned around and saw Jonathan heading straight for her on his skateboard. All she needed was to see him right now. Maybe he wouldn't say anything to her, and she could just ignore him. No such luck.

He stopped right beside Quinn's bike and flipped his skateboard into his hand.

"Hey, I see that you guys, I mean girls, are getting a little nervous," he announced.

"What?" Quinn asked, astounded. "Is that what your coach told you?"

"Well, it's true, isn't it?"

"You know, this game is getting out of control," Quinn said, getting back on her bike, and preparing to ride off. Jonathan was too quick for her, though. He grabbed her bicycle seat before she could pedal away.

"What do you mean?" he asked seriously.

She eyed him warily. "Don't you think that everyone is taking this game a little too seriously?" she asked.

"Well, yeah," he admitted. "But, it's kind of a big deal, isn't it?"

"But, it's just a game, right?" Quinn asked.

"No, it's a matter of pride," Jonathan corrected.

Quinn glanced at him, startled. He held her eyes for a moment. "You want to prove something to me, right?" he asked. She nodded. "Well, I want to prove something to you, too."

"Yeah, but . . ." Quinn began. "All these adults are taking sides, too. It's really weird. I mean, doesn't that seem like a bit much?"

"Well, my house is an armed camp. Nicole's mom wants to root for the girls, but she's afraid that it would make me mad, because, obviously, I'm playing for the boys, and my father's trying to stay right in the middle. Nicole's not talking to me at all."

Quinn shook her head. "Yeah, I can see that. It must not be any fun."

"Well, it's not. And my social studies teacher, Ms. Gorman, showed us slides of professional women athletes today, like lady bodybuilders!" Jonathan snorted.

"Welcome to the twentieth century, Stanton," Quinn teased.

"Right," he mumbled, as he scuffed his toe against the pavement. There was an awkward silence.

"So, where are you going now?" Jonathan asked quickly.

"Home," she answered, grateful for the change of subject. "Why?"

"Well, you want to give me a ride part of the way?" Jonathan asked as he let go of her seat and got back on his skateboard.

Quinn shook her head confused.

"Just pedal," he said.

She started off down the street, and he grabbed her seat again.

"You didn't tell me I had to do all the work," she accused him.

"I'm just getting you back for the pizza in my lap," he teased. She blushed. She had tried to forget about that. He hadn't.

"I am sorry, you know," Quinn apologized. "It really was an accident."

"I know, I know," he said. "I'm just busting your chops."

Quinn couldn't believe how easy it was to get along with him. This was a Jonathan she hadn't really seen before.

Too soon, it seemed to Quinn, they reached the point where she had to go straight to Nueva Beach, and he had to turn toward his house. She pulled over and stopped.

"Well, this is as far as this train goes," she said.

She had to admit that he looked great, even if he was wearing his G. Adams uniform—blue blazer, white shirt, and gray pants. She didn't see the tie anywhere. Jonathan didn't look the type to wear a tie, though.

He looked at her for a moment as if waiting for her to say something else. "Well, I guess this will be the last time I see you before the game," he said as he stuck out his hand, to shake for luck. "I probably won't see you much during the game either, so I'll see you after."

Quinn chuckled.

"What's so funny?"

Quinn thought she'd love to surprise him on the field when she walked up to play opposite him, but the moment was too good to pass up. "You'll see me all right, as soon as the game begins. I play center forward, too."

Jonathan looked totally surprised. "What?" he asked, astounded.

"I play center forward," Quinn repeated, her smile fading a little.

"This sure is complicated, isn't it?" Jonathan asked.

"What?"

"I'm going to score a lot of goals," he said matter-of-factly.

"What do you mean, you're going to score a lot of goals?" Quinn asked in an icy voice. "Don't you think that maybe I'll be able to score one or two?"

"Well, no, Quinn," he began. "I mean, you are a girl, and it's not that that's bad," he said quickly, noticing the dark look on her face, "but guys are a lot stronger and faster than you are—"

"That's what you think!" Quinn cut him off. "Why do you always have to act like you're so much better than girls? Why didn't you pay attention in social studies and wake up to the twentieth century? What's wrong with you anyway?"

"What's wrong with *me*?" he shouted back. "What's wrong with *you*? Why do you insist that girls are better than boys in sports? It's not biologically possible."

"I said as good as, not better!" Quinn shouted back. "Why are you being such a jerk about this game, anyway?"

"I'm being a jerk? What about you?"

"Me?" Quinn asked, enraged. "Well, you're really going to wake up after this game, Jonathan Stanton. After we beat you, you'll *have* to change your mind!"

"*You're* going to beat *us*? I guess we'll just have to see about that, won't we?" He jumped on his skateboard and pushed off toward his house.

"Yeah, we will!" Quinn shouted after him. "Aaargh!" she screamed loudly, as he rounded the corner. He was so frustrating, infuriating, chauvinistic . . . she could go on and on. They had been having a good time, too, until that stupid game came up. Well, she could forget about asking him to the dance. He probably wouldn't even want to talk to her now. Not that she wanted to talk to him either. She got back on her bike and pedaled slowly home.

CHAPTER 9

"It's not that I don't want to go to the dance," Nicole said, as she sat in her room with Alicia, Quinn, and Esme. "But I told you, we're going out to dinner for my grandfather's birthday. I know he'd be really upset if I canceled."

"But your grandparents like to eat early," Esme argued. "I'm sure you could be done by eight—"

"Nicole," Alicia cut in. "It will be great. We can celebrate our *victory* over the guys' team."

"All right!" Quinn exclaimed. "The power of positive thinking. We're gonna beat those G. Adams jerks on Saturday!"

"Anyway, Nicole—*Dana* will be there," Alicia teased, but stopped giggling when she saw the serious expression on Nicole's face. It was pretty obvious that Nicole didn't want to go to the dance.

"Who are you guys going with?" Nicole asked quietly, turning the attention away from her. "Did you ask anyone yet?"

"I was going to," Alicia answered quickly, "but I sort of blew it."

"What happened, Lish?" Esme asked. "Did Tyler say *no*?"

"Not exactly," Alicia said.

"Tell us!" Esme demanded.

"Well, Virginia heard from Stephanie that Jesse had already asked Tyler—"

"And he agreed to go with *her*?" Quinn interrupted. "I can't *believe* it!"

"Why didn't you ask Peter?" Esme wanted to know. "I heard from Missy that he said no to Annie Plummer because he wanted you to ask him."

"He did?" Alicia asked, trying to hide a smile.

"That's what Patty told Missy," Esme replied. "And you know Patty usually *knows*."

"Well, maybe since we *did* organize the dance together, we should kind of hang out together," Alicia said, trying to sound casual. "You know, in case there's more work to do."

"Is that the *only* reason?" Quinn asked, grinning.

"Sounds like a little romance to me," Esme said, raising her eyebrows at Alicia.

"Oh, come on, Es. You know I'm just doing my duty as class president," Alicia replied, trying to keep a straight face. "Anyway, little Miss Romance, who are *you* going with? I overheard one of the girls from your cheerleading squad say that you had a *number* of possibilities!"

"Well, not *that* many," Esme said, covering her

face with a pillow as she started to giggle.

Alicia jumped on the bed, grabbed the pillow, and started to hit her friend with it. "Tell us, or we'll have to beat it out of you," she yelled. Quinn and Nicole began to throw stuffed animals in Esme's direction.

"Okay, okay. I give up," she gasped, laughing uncontrollably. "You *know* I want to ask Bobby Turner. I've been trying to call him all week. Yesterday, I actually stayed on the phone until he answered. But then I got totally freaked out and hung up. I just couldn't make myself do it!"

"You hung up on him!" Alicia screamed. "Es, I can't believe you. Do you think he knew it was you?"

"No way," Esme replied. "He answered the phone. I didn't even have to ask to speak to him or anything. But I did hang up on his mom once, earlier in the week!"

"Esme Farrell, you are being such a major wimp!" Alicia teased. "Especially for someone who once dated an 'older' guy."

"Don't bring Gregg into this," Esme retorted.

"Anyway," Alicia continued. "I know it's hard. I totally chickened out of asking Tyler. I dialed, but I always hung up before it even started ringing."

"Hey, Es, why don't you call Bobby now?" Quinn suggested.

"Are you *kidding*?" Esme practically screamed. "You guys will totally make me laugh!"

"No we won't, Cornflake," Nicole said. "We'll just make sure you don't hang up on him again!"

"Seriously, Es, you should do it now," Alicia encouraged. "Then you won't lose your nerve."

"Okay, I will," Esme said confidently. "Let me just

find his number."

"You mean you don't know it by heart?" Quinn teased. "How many times have you dialed it?"

"You know I don't even remember *your* numbers," Esme told her friends.

"I have it right here," Alicia said. "It's on one of the class lists Peter gave me for the dance."

"Okay," Esme said, taking the number and picking up the phone. "I'm going to do this." But after she had dialed only four numbers, she began to giggle so hard she had to hang up the phone.

"Come on, Es," Nicole said seriously. "I'll dial for you."

"And I'll make sure you don't hang up!" Alicia said. "Even if I have to tie your hands behind your back."

The girls tried again, and this time Esme let it ring.

"Hello, may I please speak to Bobby," Esme said, using the professional voice she saved for speaking to her agent and magazine people. When she realized Bobby had answered the phone, she looked at her friends as if she didn't know what to say next. Alicia nudged her to speak.

"Uh, hi, B-bobby," Esme stuttered. "It's Esme."

The girls could hear a muffled answer.

"Uh, fine, I mean great," Esme answered. "How are you?" Quickly she covered the mouthpiece and looked at her friends. "What do I say now?" she mouthed to them.

"How about *asking* him," Alicia prompted. "That's why you're calling, remember?"

"He's going on and on about the soccer game,"

Esme whispered back. "Can I interrupt?"

"Ask him what he's doing *after* the game," Quinn suggested.

Esme motioned for her friends to be quiet again, and she started speaking. "I was like wondering," she began, "um, what, like, you were doing after the game?"

Esme laughed. "He said he was thinking about taking a shower," she whispered, rolling her eyes.

After a pause, Esme asked, "What about after that?" Suddenly, Alicia nudged her. "I mean, do you want to go to the Sadie Hawkins dance?" Esme quickly added.

Esme's face suddenly brightened. "Okay, I'll see you at the game," Esme said. "We can make plans then."

There was another pause. Then, Esme said, "Pizza sounds great, too. But we might be celebrating *our* victory, not *yours*."

Another long pause, and Esme answered, "We'll see tomorrow. 'Bye for now," she added as her friends stared at her in shock.

"Esme Farrell, you were *amazing!*" Alicia squealed when she had hung up. "You really told him!"

"And you're going out to dinner, too?" Nicole asked, excited for her friend.

"Not bad, huh?" Esme exclaimed, feeling proud of herself. "Who needs the phone next?" she continued, looking at Quinn, who was suddenly concentrating very hard on her social studies reading. "What about you? Who are you going with?"

"Do you guys want something to drink?" Quinn

asked, ignoring the question as she got up from the floor. "I'm really thirsty!"

"Why don't you grab a bottle of soda from the fridge," Nicole suggested. "Bring up some paper cups, and there should be a bag of cookies in the cupboard by the sink."

"All right!" Quinn exclaimed, very eager to get out of there. But as she walked down the hall she heard Jonathan and his friend Adrian coming up the stairs. He was the *last* person Quinn wanted to see just then. In fact, she'd be happy if she didn't have to see him until after the soccer game. Of course by that time, he'd probably hate her, she thought— especially if the girls *won*. But her pride stopped her from hiding from him. Nervously pushing some strands of red hair away from her face, she continued to walk toward the stairs.

"Hey, Jonathan, hi, Adrian," she said in her most confident tone of voice, giving them a shaky smile.

"Hi, Quinn," Jonathan said softly. "I didn't expect to see you before the *big game*."

"No such luck," Quinn murmured under her breath.

"What?" Jonathan asked, looking at Quinn strangely.

"Oh, nothing. I mean, why aren't you guys doing last-minute practice drills?" she stammered.

"I don't see you working up too much of a sweat either," Jonathan retorted, beginning to sound hostile again. Why couldn't he ever have a normal, friendly conversation with this girl, he wondered.

"Well, I guess we'll all be good and rested," Quinn said. "Good luck, guys."

"Yeah, you too," Adrian cut in, and he started walking toward Jonathan's room.

Quinn didn't know what to say. She wanted to say something friendly, but she didn't think she owed him any sort of apology. In fact, the more she thought about their last discussion, the angrier she got. He *had* acted like a total jerk. Jonathan just stood there staring at her. "See ya," she muttered, turning to go upstairs. When she reached the top she just stood there for a minute, breathing a sigh of relief. She went into the guest bathroom and splashed some cold water on her face, and then slowly walked back to Nicole's room.

"Hey, Quinn, where's the soda?" Esme asked.

"The *what?*" Quinn said absentmindedly.

"S-o-d-a, *soda*," Alicia spelled it out for her. "You were thirsty, remember?"

"Oh, um, yeah. I'll go get it. I mean, I forgot. I stopped in the bathroom and had a drink of water from the tap."

Esme turned to her, a confused expression on her face. Alicia just shrugged. "*Loca, muy loca,*" she exclaimed after a minute.

"I'll get some snacks," Nicole offered, and ran down to the kitchen. The room was quiet as Alicia and Esme stared at Quinn.

"So, Q, what about the dance?" Esme asked again, breaking the silence. "Are you going with anyone?"

"Actually, I hadn't really thought about it," Quinn said, trying as hard as she could to sound as if she hadn't given it any thought at all. "I've been so hyper about the game and everything, I sort of forgot about the dance. Anyway, I'm sure it will be a total bore, so I'm not going to show up for very long."

"Why won't it be fun?" Alicia asked, sounding a bit annoyed since she had worked so hard to organize it. "Don't you even want to see Jamie Farber?"

"I'm sick of him," Quinn answered, vaguely.

"Who?" Nicole asked, coming back into the room. "Is Jonathan being rude again?"

"Jonathan?" Quinn asked a little too quickly. "I didn't say anything about *him*. I just said I didn't think I'd stick around the dance too long, and that I'm *not* particularly excited about seeing Jamie Farber!"

"He's going with Virginia, anyway," Nicole said. "She actually got up the courage to ask him and he said yes."

"You're kidding!" Alicia exclaimed. "She's got guts!"

"I know," Nicole agreed. "And you'll never *guess* who Darcy invited—"

"Who?" Esme asked, hoping it wasn't any of the really cute seventh-graders.

"*Jonathan*," Nicole said. "I heard him telling Adrian before."

"What did he say?" Quinn asked immediately, and a little more eagerly than she had intended.

"I don't know, but I couldn't *believe* she asked him," Nicole said, wondering how someone could actually like her stepbrother.

"I overheard Darcy telling Vanessa she thinks Jonathan is really cute, but I never thought she'd actually *ask* him!" Esme exclaimed.

"I guess she did," Nicole said.

"Did he *accept*?" Quinn asked in an anxious voice.

"Why do *you* care so much?" Alicia asked, wondering about Quinn's sudden interest. "Don't tell me *you* were going to ask him?"

"Quinn and Jonathan?" Esme said with a grin. "That *would* be interesting!"

"Oh, come on, you guys," Quinn defended herself. "You know we're not exactly each other's number-one fans these days. Of course I don't *like* him. Be serious."

Quinn knew she was blushing. She just hoped they believed her. If only she hadn't challenged him to this stupid soccer game, she knew they'd be getting along pretty well. Then again, she really wanted to *beat* those guys. It was all too confusing!

"He didn't tell me if he was going or not," Nicole said, breaking into her thoughts. "We don't really talk about that sort of thing very much."

"Whatever," Quinn said. She really wanted to end the conversation. It was too confusing. He had been such a jerk about guys being better than girls that she really wanted to show him. So why did she want to invite him to the dance? And why did her stomach feel like doing triple somersaults when she thought about him going with Darcy Chapin? The idea of seeing them together made her completely crazy!

"I guess we'll find out Saturday night," Quinn said, trying to push her jumbled thoughts out of her mind.

"Find out what?" Alicia asked, looking up from her math homework.

"What?" Quinn asked.

"You said, 'I guess we'll find out Saturday night,' "

Alicia repeated.

"I did? I mean, I was thinking about the g-game," Quinn stuttered. "You know, we'll find out who wins by then!"

"Quinn McNair, you are in one *strange* mood today," Esme said.

"That's me!" Quinn answered, trying to make a joke out of the situation. "Wacko!" And with that, she packed up her books. She had so much on her mind that she knew she wouldn't get anything done that afternoon.

"See you guys," she called to her friends. Before they could even say good-bye, she was out the door.

CHAPTER 10

"*Caramba!* I can't believe it's raining," Alicia exclaimed as she sat in the front seat of her father's car. The day of the soccer challenge had finally arrived, and Alicia and her dad were on their way to pick up Quinn. The wipers moved slowly back and forth against the windshield as they drove along, making Alicia feel worse and worse with each stroke.

"Don't worry *muchacha bonita*. It's really only a drizzle," Mr. Antona said, trying to comfort his daughter. "Maybe it will even clear up before the game starts. It's still very early, you know."

"I hope so," Alicia groaned. But she wasn't too confident. The whole sky was gray, and the sun didn't look as if it could possibly burn through. And she was nervous! The girls hadn't really played much in the rain before. Alicia was so distracted she didn't even notice that they had arrived at Quinn's house.

"Do you want to go get her, or should I?" Mr. Antona teased, when they stopped at the McNairs'.

"Oh, sorry, *Papá*," Alicia said, jumping out of the car. "I'll be right back," she screamed as she ran up the steps to get Quinn.

"Good morning, Mr. Antona," Quinn said, trying to sound cheerful, as she got into the back seat. "Beautiful day, isn't it?" she continued, sarcastically. "But we can handle it, can't we, Lish?"

"You bet!" Alicia yelled, trying to get into the spirit. "Go PBP Go!" She reached to the back seat and gave Quinn a high five.

"I'll be rooting for you," Mr. Antona joined in, "even if I should be rooting for the *boys*."

"You better not!" Alicia screamed, before she noticed that her father was laughing. He drove on toward Palm Beach Prep, with Alicia and Quinn talking seriously about the game. Nicole and Esme were already at school for a pre-game cheerleading practice.

"See," Alicia's father said as he turned the wipers to low. "Nothing to worry about." But almost as soon as he finished his sentence, it started pouring again. Alicia looked at him out of the corner of her eye, trying not to giggle. "Okay," he admitted. "A *little* something to worry about." The three of them laughed as they pulled up by the other cars in the PBP parking lot.

"Thanks for the ride, *Papá*," Alicia said as she climbed out of the car. Luckily, the rain had slowed to a drizzle by then.

"You'll be back to watch, won't you?" Quinn asked eagerly.

"Of course I will, *chicas*," he answered. "And don't worry, you girls will give those boys what they deserve!"

"*Gracias, Papá*," Alicia said, giving her father a quick kiss on the cheek, and before Mr. Antona could say anything else, Quinn and Alicia were running toward the soccer field.

"I'm so glad the referees agreed with us about having the game here," Darcy said to Vanessa when Quinn and Alicia ran up.

"I guess Jonathan was wrong about the *professional rules*," Quinn added quietly. "Serves him right for being such a know-it-all." She had actually been thinking about Jonathan practically nonstop for the last two days, and seeing Darcy didn't help much. She was actually *going* to the dance with him, or at least she probably was. Quinn struggled to snap herself back to the present. It was almost game time, and she couldn't let that stuff bother her now! She knew that the most important thing was to try her best in the soccer game, and if that meant beating Jonathan then that's the way things would have to be. It was time to think of him as her opponent, and nothing else.

"I don't know about this rain," Chelsea said, interrupting Quinn's thoughts. "We've never had to play on such a wet field before."

"Don't worry," Coach Larsen cut in. "Just be careful not to slip. And remember, the wet grass will slow down the ball."

"Anyway," Darcy added, "the guys will have the same disadvantage. Now let's go out and do a few laps. I know the air's pretty warm, but I don't want anyone to get chilled in the rain. When you're finished running, we'll meet back here to stretch. Then we'll take some shots at goal while the guys finish their warm-up."

While the girls warmed up, lots of cars started to arrive. Most of the G. Adams team was there, hanging out near their bench, or kicking the ball around at the far side of the field. They didn't seem to be taking their warm-up as seriously as the girls were. The metal bleachers were becoming packed with parents, faculty, and students from both schools. Many people had made banners which said, "GO GIRLS!" The team members were glad that lots of people had come, but, at the same time, it made them nervous. And having Mrs. Hartman there made the game seem even more of a big deal.

Quinn looked over to where Esme and Nicole were getting ready with the rest of the cheerleaders. Nicole's moves were a little bit awkward, but she actually looked as if she were having fun. The cheerleaders were all wearing their PBP sweatshirts before the game started, so no one could see the T-shirts they had made. Esme led the girls in a final practice, modifying a few of the most difficult moves because of the slippery grass. Quinn could see the girls doing warm-up splits and cartwheels, and were finding it hard not to get too dirty or muddy. Then, as the whistle blew for the players to take the field, the girls on the squad pulled off their sweats and ran out in front of the bleachers. When the crowd saw their shirts, they went totally wild. Esme and the other girls were so happy they almost forgot what they were doing.

"Those shirts are *fantástico*," Alicia said to Quinn. "This support is really going to help us!"

"Way to go, Esme and Nicole!" Quinn yelled out, as she and Alicia watched the first cheer. It was amazing. Esme and Nicole sat on the shoulders of two seventh-graders and held up a big green and white banner that read "GO PALM BEACH PREP!!!" Four other girls stood in the line and shook huge green and white pom-poms. The remaining four girls were all on the gymnastic team and did combinations of cartwheels and round-off back handsprings. To complete the sequence, Cindy Barton and Kelly Burns did back flips. The crowd stood up and burst into wild applause. Even the G. Adams fans couldn't help clapping. The cheerleaders were really good. Then Cara and her small squad appeared, doing a series of leaps as they came out on the field. The fans started booing and hissing, and the girls' soccer team couldn't help but laugh.

"We won the toss!" Vanessa announced, as she ran in from the middle of the field to where the other girls were huddled. She and Darcy had flipped a coin with the co-captains of the G. Adams team, and the girls had won control of the ball. The girls took off their sweat suits and gathered in a circle. Joining hands in the center, they let out a loud "LET'S GO" as they raised their arms skyward. The crowd echoed their support as the girls ran onto the field and took their places. The guys were already in position and were beginning to look a bit impatient.

Quinn ran as confidently as she could to take her position opposite Jonathan.

"Hi," he said, reaching out to shake her hand.

"Hi," she replied, a little bit coldly. She was determined to concentrate on the game, and nothing else.

"Good luck," he continued, sounding sincere. "You'll need it," he added with a laugh.

"I don't think so, but thanks anyway," she answered confidently. She looked over at the ref, and waited for the whistle to start the game. When it sounded, she looked at Jonathan for a quick moment, smiled, and booted the ball backwards. Before he even knew what was happening she had gotten around him and was halfway down the field. Unfortunately, that was about as good as things got for the girls in the beginning of the game. The G. Adams forward line was really fast, and the girls were so nervous that they let two goals get by them before the end of the first quarter.

Esme and the cheerleaders started chanting, "DEFENSE—DEFENSE—DEFENSE," and the crowd joined them. As the second quarter began, the team responded to the excitement of the crowd and started playing the sort of ball that had won them the State Championship. The boys started off with the ball, but Stephanie quickly stole it from one of the G. Adams forwards. She carefully controlled the ball as she made her way upfield, frantically searching for someone to pass to. She spotted Quinn at midfield, all alone.

"Center, center," Quinn yelled, neatly receiving the pass. But Adrian had also seen Quinn, and as

soon as she had trapped the ball, he was right on
her, trying to steal it. She heard Maddy Stevens
yelling at her to pass, but it was hard enough just
keeping the ball away from Adrian. Pulling the ball
back slightly, and then tapping it ahead, she got the
ball away from him, but there was still no one to
pass to. She would have to take the ball down the
field herself. She saw a pretty open route between
herself and the G. Adams goalie, and pouring on the
speed she went straight for him.

Esme led the cheerleaders in a "GO QUINN
GO—GO QUINN GO!" cheer, with Nicole yelling
almost as loudly as Esme herself.

"C'mon, c'mon," the G. Adams goaltender confidently invited Quinn to take a shot. Quinn slowed
down several yards in front of him, and, looking
confused, the goalie moved out from the goal a little
bit to try and spook her. But before he knew what
was happening, Quinn pulled back her right foot,
and chipped the ball over his head. It landed neatly
in the right corner of the net.

The stands went wild. Quinn looked over and saw
Sean jumping up and down, screaming and cheering. As she ran back up the field to take her position,
Alicia met her and gave her a huge hug. It was only
when she had made it back to center field that
Quinn noticed Jonathan standing there, looking
serious. He took control of the ball, but the G.
Adams team had only made a couple of passes when
the ref blew the whistle, signaling halftime. It was
2–1, but the girls were definitely holding their own.

Cara and her squad ran onto the field to cheer for
the boys, but the PBP team hardly noticed. The

squad formed a kickline, and every other girl carried red and black pom-poms. The girls split into pairs, and were supposed to form an X formation, but one of the groups ran the wrong way, so no one could figure out what they were trying to do. The PBP fans weren't really interested either. They were giving their team a standing ovation, and Esme and her cheerleaders were doing a series of split-leaps and cartwheels for encouragement.

Coach Larsen called the team together to discuss strategy for the next half, but not before everyone had congratulated Quinn on her goal. Quinn was so excited about how well the game was going that she wasn't even thinking about Jonathan.

"Way to go, Quinn!" Vanessa yelled. The whole team cheered.

"You're all doing great!" the coach encouraged the rest of the team. "And now that we've played a half, I think we all understand the guys' strengths and weaknesses, so we can use some of the moves we practiced. At the beginning of the second half, look to Vanessa. She'll be signaling the plays each time we get possession.

"Just stay cool, guys," she added. "I know they've got an amazing front line, but their defense is scattered. There's no way we would have left so much of the field open the way they did when Quinn was able to score."

The girls all nodded enthusiastically. They stretched out a bit, and looked over to the guys' side. Quinn felt sick for a minute as she saw Cara's squad flirting with the entire G. Adams team. Then she pushed those thoughts out of her head and thought about the next half.

"Okay, guys, let's get psyched!" Vanessa yelled when it was time for them to take the field again. The cheers from the crowd certainly helped. The whistle blew, and the ball was in play!

This time when the half began, it was the boys who seemed a little shaky. Michael Garrett made a pass that ended up right in front of Vanessa. She quickly tapped it up the field to Alicia, who sprinted down the sideline leaving the bewildered Michael behind. Suddenly, she saw Virginia, who had left her position at halfback and moved up to the front line. Alicia passed the ball across to Nina Ellis at inner as she ran further down toward the goal. Feeling a defensive player coming at her, Nina took a shot at the goal from far out. The wet ball was heavy, and didn't lift as much as she had hoped. It was well within the reach of the goalie. But it was also hard to get a grip on. It slipped over the tops of his fingers, bounced in front of the goal line, and rolled in. The score was tied at 2–all.

The girls tried to control their excitement as they jogged back to their positions. They knew that if they kept their heads, the challenge match just might go their way. The tension and excitement of the game kept growing and growing.

After the PBP goal, the boys got control of the ball at center field. Jonathan pulled a quick fake on Stephanie, and took off down the field. Vanessa was playing fullback, and she tried to make a sliding tackle as Jonathan rushed toward her. Unfortunately, he'd seen her coming. He made a quick stop, tapped the ball over her outstretched leg, and continued downfield. The PBP halfbacks were covering the rest of the forward line pretty well, but, out of the corner of his eye, Jonathan spotted Bobby Turner sneaking down one of the sidelines. Launching an excellent pass in front of the goal, Jonathan watched as Bobby neatly guided the ball in. It was an absolutely perfect goal. Alicia looked over at Esme, who was trying to control herself from cheering for Bobby.

This time, the guys were really excited to score. They whooped and hollered for a few minutes. The girls took their positions and waited for the whistle. The drizzle was turning into a heavier downpour. Time was running out, and the girls were afraid they wouldn't get a chance to finish. One of the officials blew a whistle and the boys quickly took their places on the field once again.

There were only two minutes remaining in the final quarter, and the girls were worried. The rain was really coming down and they were still behind by one goal. When they got possession of the ball, Quinn looked to Vanessa for the play. She recognized the "sweep" signal and looked around to make sure the other girls had seen it. When the ref blew the whistle, Quinn kicked the ball to Nina, who was playing directly to her right. While all of the other girls on the forward line cut left and slowly made their way downfield, Nina and Alicia took off, once again, down the right side. They passed back and forth to avoid the one halfback who had followed them, cutting toward the goal a bit when they got near the end line. Quinn and Stephanie ran down the field at the same time. When Alicia's shot at the goal was blocked, Stephanie got control of the deflected ball, and pushed it hard past the startled G. Adams goalie. Though the girls were soaked through and through, the PBP team went out of control. They formed a massive huddle, hugging and congratulating Alicia and Stephanie. The bleachers were a sea of umbrellas and colored ponchos jumping up and down, cheering and celebrating. With the score tied at three, and only a few seconds left in the game, the guys took possession of the ball. Jonathan passed to Adrian, who started running down the left side of the field, but before he was halfway down, the whistle blew and the game was over. It only took the rain-soaked referees a few moments to decide that there would be no overtime. The girls ran off the field and were quickly surrounded by the cheerleaders and the rest of the team in a massive huddle. Everyone in the bleachers came down onto the field to congratulate them. Esme and Nicole found Alicia and Quinn, and the four girls jumped up and down, hugging.

"You did it!" Esme screamed. "You guys were great!"

"Those guys didn't know what hit them," Nicole added, excitedly.

"We couldn't have done it without your support," Alicia told her friends. "That cheerleading really got the crowd excited, and that made it so much easier for us to play."

"I bet Heartburn will let you keep the squad up full-time, if you want to," Quinn said. "You guys are *great* for school spirit!"

"I don't know about that," giggled Esme. "Can

you imagine me getting all that exercise every day?"

"Heartburn was really getting into it," Nicole told them. "I even saw her banging the stands with her umbrella!"

"*Heartburn?*" Quinn exclaimed. The thought of the serious headmistress carrying on with the rest of the fans was too much for her to imagine.

"I saw her, too," Esme confessed. "It's true. She did look pretty psyched."

"Hey!" Quinn yelled, as she felt someone grab her from behind. Struggling, she turned around and saw Sean standing there with a huge smile on his face. Quinn held up her hand and he gave her a high five. Then he grabbed her and hugged her, and tried to swing her around, but there wasn't much room in the crowd. Alicia looked and saw her parents coming toward her.

"*Mamá,*" she yelled. "Over here." Mr. and Mrs. Antona found their way over to Alicia and hugged all four of the girls.

"You were all *fantástico!*" they exclaimed.

"You guys were totally amazing!" Sean added. "I'm glad I wasn't on that G. Adams team—you women are fierce!" He backed away, pretending to be scared.

"You sure showed them!" Esme agreed.

"And Jonathan better watch what he says from now on," Nicole said confidently.

Quinn just nodded. She hadn't been thinking about Jonathan since the game ended, but as soon as Nicole mentioned his name, Quinn's stomach lurched.

"Well, we didn't actually *beat* them," she mused

out loud. "But then again, they didn't beat us either."

"I was a little worried when Bobby Turner scored that third goal," Alicia confessed. "But that sweep play really worked. They were totally fooled."

"Bobby's shot was pretty awesome," Esme said, looking over at the G. Adams team. "Maybe I should go congratulate him. You guys, does my hair look okay?"

"Well, it's a little wet," Nicole admitted. "But you look great anyway!"

Esme pulled out a tiny mirror from her sweatshirt pocket and checked herself before walking away. Alicia, Nicole, and Quinn couldn't help cracking up, because everyone looked like a total wreck after running around in the rain for so many hours. Sean was trying to control himself until Esme had gone, but he was laughing really hard, too.

"Hey, guys," Sean said, as the crowd began to disperse. "Maybe now that the game's over, it might be a good idea to get out of the rain."

"Come on, Alicia," Mrs. Antona said, putting her arm around her daughter. "You should go home and take a hot shower."

"That sounds great to me!" Nicole replied.

"Call me before you go out to dinner," Quinn said.

"Okay, congratulations again," Nicole yelled out as she jogged off to get her bike.

"I'll see you at the dance, won't I?" Alicia asked Quinn, as the Antonas headed for the car.

"Probably," Quinn said. "I'll call you."

"Okay, Q," Alicia said, knowing not to push the

subject. "Great game! I'll speak to you." The two girls hugged and Alicia ran off after her parents.

Sean picked up Quinn's bag and put his arm around her shoulder. He noticed her staring at the boys' team. A couple of them were still hanging out, and one guy was staring right back at Quinn. Sean couldn't help but notice that something was going on between the two of them.

"Why don't you go talk to him, Quinnster," Sean suggested bluntly. "It definitely looks as if he's got something to say to you."

Quinn began to smile, unable to control herself. She couldn't believe how *cool* Sean was sometimes —especially when she really needed him.

"Why don't you give me your stuff and I'll take it to the car," Sean said with a grin. "I'll wait for you there."

"Hey, Sean, thanks a lot," Quinn replied, as she handed her soccer bag over to her brother.

"No problem, *squirt*," he said, quickly jumping out of the way when Quinn kicked her soccer ball at him. He kept laughing as he ran all the way to the car.

Quinn was glad that the rest of her friends had left already. She didn't know what she would say to Jonathan, but she *knew* it would be easier if her friends weren't around. One good sign was that she hadn't seen him hanging out with Darcy at all. Maybe he didn't really like her, and maybe the rumor that they were going together to the dance wasn't true.

The remaining guys were hanging out at the far side of the bleachers. Quinn walked along the bottom row, peering down at the ground as though she was looking for something. She didn't want to make herself too obvious. As she got closer she heard bits of the conversation coming from the guys' end.

"Jonathan!" Bobby Turner exclaimed. "What's the big deal? Just tell us who your date is."

"It's for me to know and you to find out," Jonathan retorted. He began stuffing his sweats into his bag.

Quinn stopped in her tracks. So, he *was* going with someone. And he wouldn't tell the guys who it was! How could she go talk to him now? The whole thing made her so angry! Didn't he notice that they got along really well when they weren't fighting with each other?

"I'll bet she's a total dog—that's why you won't tell us," Steve Davidson said. He started running circles around Jonathan, and barking, pretending to be a dog.

"I wouldn't tell who she is, even if she looked like Madonna," Jonathan snapped. "Why would I let a bunch of jerks like you in on my social life? You've got enough problems with your own!"

"*I* have a date," Steve boasted. "And I'm not telling you anything about her."

"Good, then we're even!" Jonathan pointed out. "Quit bugging me. You'll find out at the dance won't you? Now I'm going to race you wimps to the parking lot," he said, pointing down the field.

Quinn didn't even wait to catch the end of their conversation. She pretended to pick something up from the bleachers, just in case anyone was watching. Then she sprinted back down the field until she reached the entrance to the parking lot. She stopped running and walked slowly toward the car where Sean was waiting. Moments later, the rest of the G. Adams team came running through the far end of the lot, with Jonathan a few yards ahead. Quinn got closer to the car. She hoped Sean wouldn't ask her any questions because talking was the last thing in the world she wanted to do. Jonathan had obviously agreed to go with Darcy after all. Quinn felt a definite lump forming in her throat.

What was the deal with this guy thing, Quinn wondered. Just a few months ago she had barely even thought about them. There had always been enough on her mind with school, running cross-country, seeing her friends. Now she found herself thinking about Jonathan—a lot. He was definitely confusing her life, even though she tried to be cool about it. She just didn't understand him. Sometimes he was so nice, and the next minute he was a total jerk. For a while, she had thought he might even *like* her, but now he was going to the Sadie Hawkins dance with someone else. Had she done something wrong? Obviously the article had been right about not beating the guy you like at his own game. She should never have challenged Jonathan to the soccer match. He couldn't deal with it. But then again, Darcy was on the soccer team, too.

"Earth to Quinn," Sean yelled. Quinn realized she had walked right by the car. Quickly she retraced her steps and jumped in the front seat. She gave him an embarrassed smile, and crossed her fingers, praying that he wouldn't start talking.

"How'd it go?" Sean asked, obviously not receiving her message.

"It was interesting," Quinn answered, figuring that although this wasn't as honest as telling him it was terrible, it wasn't really a lie.

"Where to, madam?" Sean asked, realizing that Quinn wasn't about to say anything else.

"Home, James," Quinn joked, and she found herself almost beginning to laugh. "To the palace," she added, with a giggle. She forced herself to think happy thoughts about how they'd almost won the soccer game and had definitely shown G. Adams a thing or two.

CHAPTER
11

"**I** wonder why Quinn doesn't want to go tonight?" Alicia asked when Esme phoned her later that afternoon.

"I don't know," Esme answered. "She's been acting really strange lately. Do you think she was too chicken to ask someone?"

"Are you kidding?" Alicia exclaimed. "Quinn's got more guts than anyone I know. Do you think she'd wimp out about asking some guy?"

"You're right," Esme agreed. "She'd ask anyone she wanted. So what do you think is bothering her?"

"I don't know. I know she was uptight about the game," Alicia said, "but I thought she'd cool out when it was over—especially after we did so well!"

"Well, maybe she'll surprise us and show up. Anyway, Lish, what are you wearing?" Esme asked, turning the conversation over to one of her favorite subjects—clothes.

"I think I'm going to wear my navy-blue miniskirt with that pale pink sweatshirt, and my pink loafers. You know Peter, he's kind of conservative."

"I *love* those loafers!" Esme exclaimed. "You'll look great. I just wish *I* could decide."

"I'd love to see your room right now," Alicia said, giggling, knowing what a mess Esme made when she was trying to figure out what to wear. "Do you have stuff *everywhere?*"

"Everywhere!" Esme answered, looking around her room at the piles of clothes on the bed, the floor, and her desk chair. "Right now I have on my new jeans—you know, the ones with rips down the fronts of both legs. I'm wearing these awesome fuchsia tights underneath, which you can see through the tears."

"That sounds so cool," Alicia cut in. "What are you wearing on top?"

"Just a plain white T-shirt, and this fuchsia bolero jacket I got last week at that *YM* shoot," Esme answered, stepping over three piles of clothes to look at herself in the mirror hanging from her closet door. "But I think I'm going to change. I'm not sure it's the right look for a PBP dance, are you?"

"Come to think of it, I'm not sure Heartburn would be too big on ripped jeans," Alicia said.

"Yeah, I guess you're right," Esme agreed, "even though she has the worst fashion sense of anyone I know! Can you imagine what she'd say if I told her these jeans are the coolest new thing?"

"Can you imagine her *wearing* a pair?" Alicia

added, giggling, trying to imagine Mrs. Hartman in any sort of jeans. "So what are you going to change into?"

"I'll surprise you," Esme said, and then, hearing her mother knock on the door, whispered, "Lish, I have to go. If I don't make this room look neat in the ten seconds before Mom comes in she's going to kill me! And I'd rather live, at least until after my date with Bobby Turner."

"Okay, Es, I'll see you at the dance," Alicia said. "Have fun with Mr. Gorgeous until then!"

"You, too," Esme said. "Bye."

Alicia heard the phone click before she even had a chance to say good-bye. She dialed Quinn's number and let the phone ring at least ten times. Finally a grumpy voice snapped, "Hello."

"Hi, is Quinn there?" Alicia asked, quickly.

"Lish?" Quinn replied. "It's me."

"I didn't even recognize your voice, Q," Alicia said, starting to giggle. "What's with you?"

"I just didn't feel like getting the phone," Quinn said, "and no one else is home."

"What's the matter?" Alicia wanted to know.

"Nothing," Quinn answered immediately. "I mean, I'm *exhausted*, that's all."

Alicia didn't feel very hopeful about getting Quinn to come to the dance, but she thought she'd give it one more try. "Are you going to come celebrate?" she asked, cheerfully.

"Lish, I think I'm just going to make it an early night," Quinn answered. "But I'm sure you'll have a great time."

"You really won't go?" Alicia said.

"Lish, I'm really beat. If I change my mind I'll see you there, okay? But now it's nap time, big time!"

"Okay, Q. You win. But *try* to change your mind. I better go meet Peter, I guess. It wouldn't be too cool if I were late."

"Have fun," Quinn said, trying to sound cheerful. "See ya."

"Bye," Alicia said, a little sadly. She hung up the phone and looked in the mirror. She thought her outfit was really cute. Just because Quinn was sulking didn't mean she couldn't have a good time, did it? She ran down the hall to the kitchen where her mom was waiting to drive her over to PBP.

Quinn sat up quickly and looked at the clock. It was a quarter to eight. The Bob Marley record that had been blaring when she fell asleep had stopped playing, and it was almost dark outside. She couldn't believe she had just slept for two hours, especially with the volume of her record turned almost all the way up! She went into the bathroom and splashed some cold water on her face and looked in the mirror. Not thinking about anything for a few hours definitely had done her a lot of good.

Wait a minute, she thought. We did really well today! Why am I at home alone, sulking? Then she remembered—Jonathan. Suddenly, she got mad. How could she lie there and feel sorry for herself? It was boring first of all, and feeling this way about some guy certainly wasn't worth it! Quinn loved music and she loved to dance. Why shouldn't she just go and have fun with her friends? So what if Jonathan was going with Darcy? She could still have a good time—with her friends. Quickly, she picked up the phone and dialed Nicole's number.

"Hi, Nicole?" Quinn said, as soon as Nicole got to the phone. She was relieved that Nicole was back from dinner with her grandparents. "How was dinner?" she asked.

"It was delicious!" Nicole said. "I ate so much I think I'm going to burst. That cheerleading sure gave me an appetite!"

"Well, how about some more celebrating," Quinn suggested cheerfully.

"What do you mean?" Nicole wanted to know. "I couldn't eat another thing."

"I didn't mean food," Quinn explained. "I thought it would be fun if we headed over to the dance. It's only about eight o'clock, so there's plenty of time!"

"Oh, I don't know, Quinn," Nicole said, hesitantly. "I'm kind of tired. And without Jonathan around, it's quiet for once!"

"You mean you'll let *him* go celebrate how well the guys did, and you won't celebrate how well the *girls* did?" Quinn demanded. "Come on, it'll be fun."

"What would I wear?" Nicole asked quietly. Quinn couldn't believe what she was hearing. Nicole interested in clothes? "Nicole Whitcomb, I can't believe *you* are asking *me* what you should wear. You look good in everything, anyway. How about those tapered maroon pants, and that really cool polka-dot shirt your mom got you?"

"Okay. And I can get the driver to pick you up on the way if you want," Nicole said, beginning to get excited about the dance.

"That would be great!" Quinn exclaimed. "He wouldn't mind driving all the way over here?"

"It's not that far," Nicole reminded her.

"Awesome!" Quinn declared with a giggle. "Just honk when you get here."

"Okay, I'll see you in about twenty minutes," Nicole said and hung up the phone.

Quinn looked around the room. She knew exactly what to wear because she had thought about it when she imagined that she might go to the dance with Jonathan. She ran over to her closet and pulled out her black stretch pants. Then she found her new royal-blue rayon T-shirt. She tucked it into the pants and put on a black belt with a big silver buckle. Her pants fit neatly into her low, lace-up black boots. As she looked in the mirror, she liked what she saw. The blue shirt really made her eyes stand out, and the pants were much more flattering than her usual baggy ones. It was definitely a cool outfit. She went into the bathroom, brushed her teeth, ran a comb through her thick red hair, and tried on the black hairband her mom had given her. It was sort of ·prissy, she thought, but why not?

Before she knew it, she heard a car honk outside. She ran downstairs and, as she looked in the hall mirror, she pulled off her hairband. It just wasn't her, after all, she decided. She scribbled a note to Sean, and then went outside to where Nicole was waiting. Nicole actually looked sort of excited, and suddenly Quinn felt great. Who cares about guys, she thought. I'm going to have a fun time anyway!

CHAPTER 12

"**W**ow! Look at this place!" Quinn exclaimed as she and Nicole walked into the dance. "This is *amazing!*"

"These colors are incredible," Nicole added, looking around. Alicia and the middle school dance committee had done a great job decorating the PBP gym. They hadn't known what to do for a Sadie Hawkins theme, so they just decided to make everything really bright and festive. Alicia had found a store that made neon-colored helium balloons, and she had let them loose in clusters all over the ceiling of the gym. The committee had tied brightly colored ribbons that hung down from the balloons. The stall bars were covered with streamers, and the refreshment tables had multicolored tablecloths on them.

A DJ was playing music at maximum volume, and

although, as usual, there were girls on one side of the room and guys on the other, there were quite a lot of people dancing.

"Oh, wow, look over there," Quinn yelled to Nicole over the noise of the music. A banner on the far wall had just caught her eye. It read, "CONGRATULATIONS MIDDLE SCHOOL SOCCER TEAM— 1989 FLORIDA STATE CHAMPS."

"Not bad!" Nicole yelled back.

"Hey, let's find Alicia and Esme," Quinn suggested.

"I think I see Esme and Bobby dancing over there," Nicole said, pointing across the room.

"That's Es, all right. Look at those pants. They're wild," Quinn exclaimed. Esme had decided on baggy white jeans that were about three sizes too big, but with the brown belt that held them up at the waist they looked really cool. The belt matched her low brown boots perfectly, and her cropped orange T-shirt practically glowed in the dark.

"Let's go over there," Nicole yelled, as she started pushing through the crowd on the dance floor. They passed Jesse and Patty dancing together. Quinn wondered what had happened to Tyler, Jesse's supposed date, whom she'd been bragging about all over the place.

Esme spotted Nicole and Quinn and waved excitedly. "I can't believe you guys showed up," she squealed. "This dance is totally great," she continued, beaming at Bobby, who looked like he was having just as much fun as she was.

"Have you seen Lish?" Quinn asked.

"Not in a while," Esme answered. "I saw her

dancing up a storm with Peter before, and I think I even spotted her dancing with *Tyler.*"

"I guess we should find her," Nicole said, realizing that they should probably leave Esme and Bobby alone for a while.

"Yeah, let's go this way," Quinn agreed. "See ya later, Es."

"Mom's coming at ten-thirty if you guys need a ride," Esme yelled after them as they walked away.

"Cool! Thanks a lot," Quinn shouted back, and then continued to push through the crowd. "I know you've eaten," she said to Nicole, "but I'm starving! Do you mind if we go invade the potato chips?"

Before Nicole had a chance to answer, she felt someone tap her on the shoulder. She turned around to see Cliff Barnett standing there holding a cup of soda. "Champagne for the lady?" he asked, with a grin. Nicole took the soda from his hand because she didn't know what else to do, and she certainly didn't know what to say. Quinn, noticing that Nicole was no longer right behind her, turned around and saw Nicole standing there looking stunned. Quinn winked, and then walked away.

When she reached the far side of the dance floor, something suddenly came to Quinn's attention. In the corner of the gym she saw Darcy, but she wasn't dancing with Jonathan—she was dancing with Adrian Randolph! So where was Jonathan? Quinn's stomach began to tie itself in knots once again. She grabbed a handful of Cheeze Doodles, but felt herself rapidly losing her appetite. She didn't really feel like celebrating anymore.

"Nice playing in the soccer game," a voice from

nearby said. Quinn turned to see Cara, Mimi, Jesse, and Patty standing a few feet behind her. "I guess you just didn't have what it takes to win," Cara continued. "Too bad, after all the bragging you did!"

"We gave it our best," Quinn said calmly, trying to control her temper. "And the only bragging I heard was you and your traitor cheerleading squad. I think it's pretty sick that you rooted against your own school!"

"I wouldn't have been on Esme's stupid squad if you paid me!" Cara snapped back. "She doesn't know anything about cheerleading anyway."

"Her cheerleading squad was incredible," Quinn said, trying not to let her voice shake with anger. "Until Es and the rest of the cheerleaders got the crowd going, we weren't psyched at all. When they got started, the team played so much better!"

"It didn't look like such a great game to me," Cara began, turning to her friends and laughing. "And it certainly didn't seem like the G. Adams guys were trying very hard—"

"We were trying *very* hard," a voice interrupted, and Quinn gulped as she saw Jonathan walk up next to her. "The girls played a better game then *I* ever thought they could," he continued. The smile quickly left Cara's face.

"Oh, I know, I was just kidding," Cara said after an awkward moment of silence. "Congratulations, Quinn," she added with a smirk, and then quickly walked away, followed closely by Mimi, Patty, and Jesse.

Quinn turned to face Jonathan. Again she felt at a loss for words, something she was getting used to feeling around him. After a moment she stuttered, "Uh, thanks a lot."

"I meant it," Jonathan said sincerely. "I couldn't believe it. And I'm sorry, Quinn. You guys were fantastic."

"We *girls,*" Quinn said and then laughed to herself. She couldn't believe how he was rambling on and on.

"Oh, um, yes. You *girls* were fantastic," Jonathan quickly corrected himself. "You want to dance?"

"Uh, sure," Quinn said. Once again he had taken her by surprise. She hadn't danced at all since she had gotten there, and she suddenly really felt like dancing. They danced to a couple of really good songs, and then a slow song came on. They looked at each other. "You want to go over to the water fountain?" Quinn asked. "I'm *really* thirsty."

"Sure," Jonathan answered. Quinn wondered if she was imagining things or if he looked a bit upset. She followed him across the dance area to the water fountain at the back of the gym. They walked right by Esme and Bobby, but Esme didn't seem to notice.

"Nice outfit, McNair," Jonathan commented when they were in the better-lit part of the gym. "What happened to the black high-tops?"

"I don't wear them *all* the time," Quinn answered, thinking that Jonathan was making fun of her again.

"I know. I was just trying to compliment you," he answered.

"Oh, thanks," Quinn said, realizing that she had overreacted a little. There was another awkward silence, so Quinn looked around the gym.

"Are you looking for someone?" Jonathan asked,

casually. "Who did you come here with anyway?"

Quinn swallowed hard. Would he think she was a loser if she told him she didn't have a date? "Um, uh, a friend," Quinn said, mysteriously. "By the way," she added, changing the subject, "what happened to Darcy?"

"How'd *you* know I was going with Darcy?" Jonathan asked, looking surprised.

"Rumor had it," Quinn said with a smile.

"Actually," Jonathan told her quietly, "it turned out that she really wanted to ask Adrian, but he had already told Kelly that he'd go with her, even though he didn't really want to."

"Did you want to go with Darcy?" Quinn asked, hoping she wasn't asking too many questions.

"I had nothing better to do, and no one else asked me. Darcy's okay," he answered. "What about your mystery date? Why did you ask him?"

"Actually it was a *girl,*" Quinn said very seriously. "Her name's Nicole Whitcomb."

"You came with Nicole!" Jonathan almost screamed. "I didn't even think she was coming."

"I talked her into it," Quinn replied. "I wasn't going to go at all because I couldn't think of anyone to ask, but I changed my mind at the last minute," she continued. She was beginning to feel funny about the whole thing again. Jonathan hadn't said that he didn't like Darcy, so maybe he did. She tried to walk away. But Jonathan grabbed her hand and pulled her back.

"Chill out, will you? I wasn't trying to start a fight. I think it's great that you and Nicole decided to come," Jonathan said.

"Oh," Quinn managed to say, very aware that Jonathan hadn't let go of her hand. She wondered if she would completely lose her ability to speak if he kept holding it.

Luckily there was a distraction at the front of the gym. Alicia and Peter had just unrolled a huge colorful banner which read, "GIRLS 3—BOYS 3" and below it, "CONGRATULATIONS!"

"You deserve that," Jonathan said, squeezing Quinn's hand. "Let me congratulate you."

"You mean it?" Quinn asked, sounding surprised that he was being so nice.

"I'm not a *total* jerk," he answered seriously.

"Just some of the time," Quinn teased.

"Is that why you didn't want to ask *me* to the dance—because of all that obnoxious stuff I was saying?" Jonathan asked.

"Not exactly," Quinn said very quietly.

"So you thought about it?" Jonathan said.

"I never said *that*," Quinn protested halfheartedly.

"So you *didn't* want to ask me," he said in a disappointed voice.

"Well, I never said that either. I mean I did, but then I thought, you, like thought that . . ." Quinn couldn't believe she was having so much trouble talking. Her brain just wasn't functioning.

"I think I get it," Jonathan said, looking seriously at Quinn.

"Anyway," Quinn said, recovering her composure, "congratulations are in order for you, too."

"Thanks," Jonathan said, still looking at her. Suddenly, he leaned over and quickly kissed her on the lips. Quinn became totally flustered. She could tell that Jonathan was smiling, but she also wondered if every other person in the room had seen him kiss her. How totally embarrassing! She glanced around nervously, but luckily everyone was still giving their attention to Alicia and Peter. She looked back at Jonathan and smiled. Then, as the music started, she looked around the room again to see who was dancing. She was pretty relieved when she saw Esme, Alicia, and Nicole walking over to them.

"Quinn," Alicia squealed. "I'm so glad you changed your mind about this dance. Isn't it fun?"

"Where have you been, anyway?" Nicole asked. "I've been looking for you ever since I escaped from Cliff."

"You didn't look like you were trying too hard to escape," Esme teased.

"I was so," Nicole defended herself.

"Quinn," Jonathan interrupted, "I'll be right back, I've gotta go talk to Adrian for a minute. See you guys later, he added, waving to Nicole, Alicia, and Esme.

"What was *that* about?" Esme asked as soon as Jonathan was out of sight.

"It looked like you guys were having a pretty fun time," Alicia said, with a teasing grin. "I thought you two were supposed to be enemies!"

"Well, I was trying to be a good sport," Quinn replied quickly. "Besides, you guys weren't exactly being good company. I mean Esme only had eyes for Bobby, and Alicia had disappeared somewhere with Peter, and Cliff had kidnapped Nicole. What else could I do?"

Alicia looked from Nicole to Esme and then back to Quinn before she burst out laughing. Nicole and Esme quickly joined her.

"You guys!" Quinn exclaimed. "Don't we deserve to celebrate?"

Her three friends were laughing so hard they couldn't answer. After a few moments they saw Jonathan coming back toward them.

"I think that's our cue," Esme said between giggles.

"Time to disappear!" Alicia added.

"See you later," Nicole said, grinning.

And before Quinn had a chance to reply, her three friends had left. Her favorite Ziggy Marley song started playing as Jonathan walked up.

"Perfect timing," he said, as he took Quinn's hand and led her out onto the dance floor.

Watch for SCREEN TEST
next in the Palm Beach Prep series
coming soon from Tor Books

"You guys," Esme Farrell exclaimed, running up to where the three girls were standing in the hallway by their lockers. "I have the most incredible news! You'll never believe it!"

Esme flipped her white-blonde braid over her shoulder and paused dramatically while Alicia, Nicole, and Quinn looked at her. They were used to Esme's dramatics by now. After all, Esme never let them forget that she planned to be a famous actress when she grew up, although at the moment she settled for being a model. With her white-blonde hair and gorgeous blue eyes, Esme was undeniably beautiful.

"Well, what's your incredible news?" Quinn asked Esme impatiently. "Wait, let me guess, Heartburn's retiring?"

"Heartburn will never retire, Quinn," Nicole said in a mock-serious tone, her brown eyes sparkling. "She *is* PBP."

"Can you imagine what it would be like without her, Quinn?" Alicia asked teasingly. "You'd miss her." She tossed her thick, black curls off her face and tied them back with a green scarf.

"You're right," Quinn agreed. "I wouldn't know what to do with my afternoons." Quinn was trying to play as serious as Nicole, but her laughing blue eyes gave her away.

"You guys!" Esme shouted, exasperated. "Don't you want to hear my news?"

The three of them stopped talking and stared at Esme.

"Well . . ." Alicia prodded Esme.

"Come on, Es, spit it out," commanded Quinn. "I have to answer the royal summons."

"Really," echoed Nicole.

"I got an agent in Hollywood and—" Esme began.

"*Caramba!*" Alicia exclaimed. "Hollywood!"

"Lish, let me finish," Esme commanded. "And, I'm going to California for a screen test next week!"

"A screen test?" Quinn asked, excitedly. "That's great!"

"*Ay!*" Alicia yelled. "Esme, you *are* going to be a movie star!"

"Just like you always wanted," Nicole cried, happy for her friend. "But, what about the school fair? You'll be back for it, won't you?"

"Bobby Turner would kill you if you weren't," Alicia teased. The annual sixth-grade school fair was held with G. Adams Prep, PBP's brother school. It was definitely a social highlight and a not-to-be-missed event.

"That's a couple of weeks away, Nicole!" Esme exclaimed. "How can you worry about that already? I'm going to Hollywood. I might meet River Phoenix or Tom Cruise or somebody else. Aren't you guys excited for me?'' She paused for breath, and finally got her combination to work. Her locker popped open, spilling books, papers, and clothes everywhere.

"Tom Cruise!" Alicia breathed. "Can you imagine? He's gorgeous!"

"What would I say to him?" Esme wondered, sorting through the pile on the floor in front of her locker.

"I hope you'd say 'hi,' Es," Quinn kidded.

"Quinn!" Esme scolded, putting back her gym clothes, and picking up her books. "I'm serious!"

"I know, I know," Quinn appeased, helping Esme hold everything in, as she quickly slammed the locker door shut. The four girls moved on to Quinn's locker.

"We're talking Tom Cruise here," Esme said. "This is totally serious."

"If Esme becomes a star," Nicole mused later to Alicia, pulling a book out of her ultra neat locker, "do you think she'll have to move to Hollywood?"

"*Ay!*" Alicia exclaimed. "I never thought of that. That would be terrible!"

Nicole silently agreed as she shut her locker and followed Alicia to their French class.